LATE MARRIAGE
PRESS

HELEN BONAPARTE

a novel

SARAH D'STAIR

LATE MARRIAGE
PRESS

ISBN:

Private Printing 2021 by Late Marriage Press

for M.

HELEN
BONAPARTE

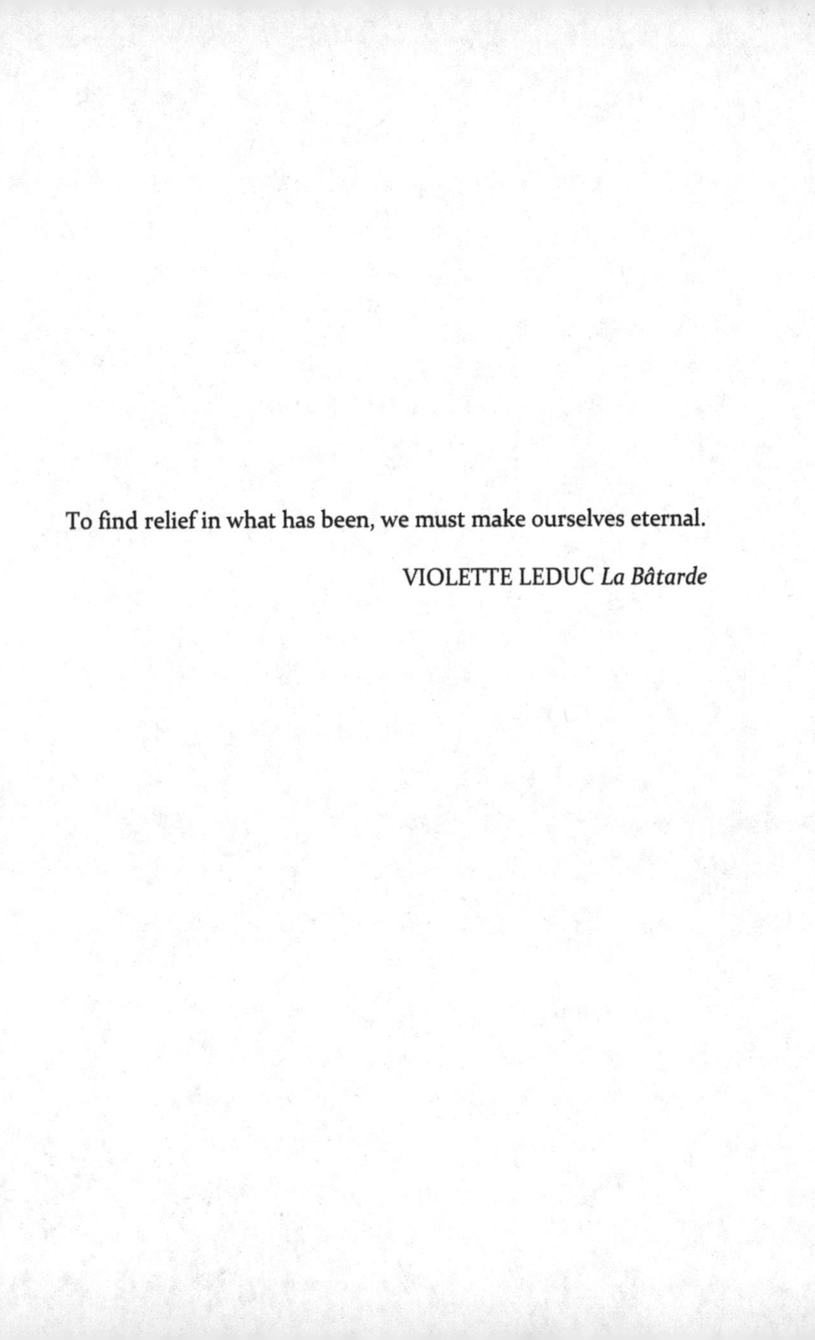

To find relief in what has been, we must make ourselves eternal.

VIOLETTE LEDUC *La Bâtarde*

Day One
Arrival

VENICE. UNFORTUNATE CITY.

Airport slumber in our eyes, we begin the first grey day. A water taxi speeds us down the open waterway while innocuous orange buoys taunt their way ahead of us. Knees collect center stage. We crane our necks to watch buildings grow menacing in the tiny front window.

My hands search for somewhere to rest. The suitcase is out of reach. I cannot find a trace of pocket. This space is filled with strange hands, strange lips, bared smiling teeth and throated voices. Six young girls are my company this week on an eight-day tour of Italy. I note the irony of youth in a water taxi as I struggle for warmth next to an upturned nose at the state of my tattered raincoat.

We are carried across the Venetian landscape through the city proper, a stream of hands across an ancient roulette wheel. I am the new one here. I sit awkward, participate in clipped smiles and nodded gestures. Feats of imagination are being lost along the way. Waves fragment, disassociate themselves ahead of me.

A short walk past the taxi drop-off leads to the hotel. Once inside, a prim Italian man speaks English and places a large door key in my hand. Heavy, dusty stairs lead to rooms that line the hall. I remark my love of hotel rooms layered with surreptitious cigarettes, stolen scent on fingertips, worn carpets that mildew your toes and feet, crisp sheets pulled flat, long showers in hot water.

This is the first hotel room of the week, a large white room with royal blue trim, blue carpet, light blue shutters, blue, blue, a television hung on the wall. It is mine for the night. The walls grow up around me, pull me into their breath. They say, You're welcome. I nurture the silence, hear footsteps that just as soon vanish. Bathroom tiles cool my bare feet, a towel-warmer fascinates and upends expectations. Not a luxury, but a patience, and a pointed toe. These doors bring you in warm for a while, then expel you into lined itineraries on paper you have not yet touched.

I head downstairs, must not be late for dinner. Downstairs is what I want to be a dream, to feel like Art. Instead, it is an overdone eye for detail, a rococo aesthetic thick with white lace and pink flowers, an every-item-for-sale sort of room. The pincushion sofa, the marble vase, the bouquet of artificial flowers, price tags mope down their sides. I sit on the chair labeled discount. The word has no compunction.

A sofa and a chair face me empty. I remark how it comes to me sometimes, emptiness. Empty chair, empty wine bottles sit here with me in silence and pay attention to the words I would say, destroy me in this chair. From here the curtains appear solid in damp light, the stairs carpeted in rosemary, the room just behind my back filled with secrets and stolen teacups.

The quiet lasts as long as my breath, as long as it takes for the hotel attendant to hang a gold key on a silver hook. The silence bites down, swallows the sound of two female voices, cat-scratched voices, voices that burn your tongue, voices that break the lamp to a shatter. These women will also be with me here for the week, tour mates from a small Texan town, they are ready to paint the whole of Italy with their flaccid brushes.

I tell myself to still my tongue, to make room for theirs, except that is a habit I am here to break.

I hear broken tires on a long flat roadway, broken nail tips, broken fields of vision as a large round body stands just in front of my swollen ankles. These women wear blue cardigan sweaters that barely wrap over their breasts, tugged tight all evening. There is a clear hierarchy here. Only a fallen civilization would produce such women, large in their wallets and conversations. I respond to them only twice all evening while they reveal that vapid enjoyment of Dante and Austen peculiar to secondary school English teachers.

The words these women decide to say are the torn flesh of my aching foot, they inspire loathing, fat fingered hands full with gigantic cell phones. They cross their legs when they sit, talk to two people at once, claim to know about Charles Dickens, say they've read Tennyson. They complain about film versions of novels and labor offensively to find words. They care only about periods and quotation marks. Yes, quotation marks are all they know, all their eyes see suspended before them. They sit next to me, inform the space and the silence.

A week of these women among Italian monuments and skylines painted yellow. The architecture of the gods is not in this room. I may find it in Assisi. Right now, I am a pot of boiled water licking the surface of my own skin.

The hotel sitting room fills with large bellies and crackling toes, hiccoughs and rolled eyes. Rolled cigarettes not yet lit, the smell of pleurisy, water and alcohol in deep-veined blood that stops just before the heart.

Then.

Marieke.

A grand celebration.

The tour guide, Marieke, descends the stairs.

I will know her too for one week. Just now, her voice spins in another direction, offers instructions I cannot hear. She does not see me at all. My body is pierced with Marieke.

In the crowded room, I see proof that visions are real,

creeping along stairs we've hidden under, fumbling with keys, mispronouncing words over a mocking telephone line. I hear a deep breath next to me. A man has taken his place, his stomach near my face. A smell of someone lost, a lost tongue, eyes that glaze sympathetic out old factory windows, fingers wrapped around a woman's hand. This man is burned hands like me. I cannot fathom his stomach. Luckily, his belt stops the sagging masses.

PATRICIA HIGHSMITH'S SEVERE gaze and wide mouth are with me here in Italy, her words and cigarettes whisper in the dark. She keeps the pencil moving, relaxes the cheeks and nose.

Last night I was wrinkled brows at the bookshelf. Marcel's voice asks, Where are you going again? Venice, Florence, Rome? Yes, I say. He says, Highsmith. An obvious choice. A finger pluck to book spine draws the novel down, he offers me *Those Who Walk Away*. This one takes place in those towns I think, he says. Venice, Rome, yes. Highsmith in Italy with six girls and two loud women. It seems almost obscene, such tense exchanges and thudding prose in Italy. The world infused with Highsmith's pulse, a hand resting on a hotel door, a pulled trigger, a tipped hat turned to footsteps, suitcase handles, voices over a distant telephone line.

Marcel tends to know the perfect book, just the right music to run the fingers through. He can be counted on for a word or a nod, whichever suits the moment. He is the consolations of philosophy and Plato's incessant questions, frail lines of cigarette smoke, haunted churches of Ireland, streets of Paris from in my dreams. He is the father of the two children we have together whom I left at home with my university briefcase. He is the hands that know card tricks and how to draw faces, the voice that reads Moby Dick aloud, suit coats the boys wish they were big enough to wear. We are in the habit of watching old horror films, we find the voices within them illuminating.

Marcel and Highsmith are with me this week. Marcel is the prose, she is the book pages that bleed out my kindling obsession with Marieke. Marieke, she is the image. Our tour guide for the week, long blonde hair that curls at its ends. I will want to warm her cold hands with my breath.

Marieke. She tells us to follow her into the dark Venetian night, across the street and to the water, enclose ourselves with her in a small, checkered-tablecloth restaurant. Her long green sweater jacket reaches almost to the ground. The skin on her ankles bristles at the top of her shoes, her calves flex as she walks out in front of the line, timid breezes carry strands of her hair in all directions. They too have just become aware of her, vaguely desire to touch her softly enough to conceal the caress that has taken shape over her body.

She leans back to open the restaurant door wide, moves several inches closer to me. I note the length precisely. I wonder, will I be aware of the space between us all week? I think of questions to ask her that are increasingly personal. Highsmith would likely see me from across the room and smile.

TWELVE ADULTS SIT at the dinner table with me. Marieke moves between tables, greets each guest in long direct looks, places her slim hand on several large shoulders. I quickly hide the fat on my belly under the table. I think, Her teeth are so white they can't be trusted. I please myself with phrasework.

Perhaps she will make her way to me soon. After all, the seat next to me left itself purposefully empty. If all goes well, her ceremonies will end with me when she sits to eat her meal.

The restaurant drowns in half smiles, full glasses of wine, stale bread, yesterday's raindrops still clinging to the wall. The overwhelmed coat rack rests politely near the tabletop. I must keep my feet still.

She saves me for last, slowly makes her way to me, sits in the seat just at the end of the table. Her body is immediately to my left.

There must be no confusion about my intentions. I should have packed nicer clothes, more than this uniform of worn blue jeans and black t-shirt, the result of many anxious decades deciding what to wear. I am dull next to her bright blond hair, her laugh, her large hoop earrings. My clothes rattle their cages.

She speaks Italian to the waiter, orders me a vegetarian meal. Her voice asks me, Is that okay?

Of course, yes.

She enters a dream with me while the restaurant noise tenses with inebriation. I touch my short hair, shaved only two months prior. The length inspires me, like a glimpse into a nighttime window. My excitement at the flitting thought of her hair on my shoulder compels me to speak a word in Italian. Her laugh tries to understand. My hands become fools, reach for the water glass, tap instead fork to plate. She pretends not to notice.

In anticipation of this week, I devour long strands of pasta and grind cheese between my teeth, imagine Marieke's voice sent out over ancient alleyways. I listen to details of her life—her Roman apartment, Dutch parents, Master's degree in Art History, refusal to ingest animal flesh, insistence that this will be the last tour she gives. I tell her I got here just in time, then.

Her hands are now only inches away from the bread that will soon be in my mouth. A film of oil from her lipstick lingers on the wine glass. Her hair might brush over my arm if I time it just right.

My tone during the conversation is one of polite obsession, the kind hidden in bedclothes and between the pages of books, buried in fingernail clippings you trim just in case, thoughts of the top of her foot bare in the twilight street shadow. I must decide now how far I will indulge myself. Shall I allow my eyes to rest a moment too long? Is her discomfort important, or is my shadow? Shall my gestures of interest be the ones in a Highsmith novel, or simply a set piece for atmosphere along Venetian bridges and swollen storefronts? I may get to touch her shoulder if I am careful. She may sit near me again, but for now, I must reveal only the slightest eye movement, and allow her into what I know of Dante.

Marieke, the student of art who claims she is no artist. She will become the story I decide her to be. Her long green sweater will guide my walks along dark city streets, I will watch carefully the strands of hair that catch her earrings and her lips, that relax over her breasts. She has just asked me a question. The answer is uninteresting, a slow drawl of words I spell out with the intention of becoming just anonymous enough not to draw attention. Eventually, she must resume her duties as tour guide.

The restaurant empties itself of conversation, night follows us back to the hotel. The water is still, waves have forgotten their purpose, dim streetlights disappear into the black sky. Her smile guides us across the street of our deep fatigue, guides us into slumber.

My body, bath water, channels of Italian TV, they lull me to sleep with their temptations, weight of eye on a tired night, quiet of a solitary hotel room key left in the door lock. The night outside whispers its secrets through closed shutters. A voice calls out the wrong name, the wrong telephone line echoes into tomorrow.

I close my eyes with bored fatigue. Memories of today will take shape while I sink into the gaze of this over-sized bed, linger for a moment, consider tomorrow's itinerary. Castle, museum, clock tower, streets, bridges, bodies, boats, gold earrings, blond hair, a blindfold held out to me, the day a slow crawl toward the long shadow of evening.

Day Two
Venice

MORNING FEELS LIKE a distant memory. My shabby jacket hangs over me, oversized as melancholy. Helen and her grand black raincoat with holes for pockets.

Today, our group will trade one garish lobby for another, one guarded castle for another, my raincoat for a dusty canvas on a palace wall. We follow Marieke single file all the way to the water taxi. I sit inside with a dozen others in long straight rows, but the young girls stay outside, wind lashing their indulgent skin.

The week has just started. There will be plenty of time for Marieke, to hear the abstraction of her lips parting into a smile, to see finger touch to hair. She takes us to Saint Mark's Square where we are joined by a new tour guide for the morning. I had heard of this new tour guide over breakfast while Marieke's legs bent slightly toward her oranges and yogurt.

We walk along a clouded morning sky to the water, then to Doge's Palace just to the side of the Square. Marieke says, This is Saint Mark's Square, with the air of stolen kisses. Her eyes glance over columns and tiles, artist hands all over me.

The new tour guide joins our circle, speaks Italian with Marieke. I lose track of the conversation. Her short black leather jacket takes over, vaguely down to her waist. She wants to learn our names and so formulates a silly game, an invasive maneuver. We are to pair our names with some unique trait of ours. She says by way of example, My name is Lucia and my favorite animal is a Lion. L and L, you see?

The alphabet attacks the morning, on a sidewalk in Venice at 8:54 am.

We go around the circle and I cannot think of a single trait of interest involving myself, nothing anyway that I would care to share. My hand reaches toward anxiety, the dark fear of being uninteresting to even the most boring of human beings. An untenable state.

What did I say when it was my turn? What can I remember saying? I remember. I said, My name is Helen. I am a Greek Goddess.

I hear the Texan's nervous laughter. The castle bloats the square, my body too takes up space. Pant cuffs trend too close to the ankles, my waistline digs deep into a protruding belly. I had tried to lose five pounds, perhaps I knew she would be here. But now, my bloated jeans and shabby raincoat stare inherently at this new tour guide whose name begins with Lion.

A semi-circular order of faces pointed in her direction, we wait for 9:00 when the bronze statues atop the tower will swing their hammers to ring the clock bell. I am less interested in the clock tower than in my worn brown shoes, bought at a shop in Ireland with Dierdre. I fear they'll become less an icon and more a mutiny. I can hardly bear the thought of it, the mistrusted weight of packed leather.

We wait for the bell for two more minutes. Our toes rustle in our shoes, eyes liquid pastels on a faint canvas, hollow as fingers that fly over telephone cameras. Amid all of this, I am masked into a question, from a stranger.

Have you heard the clock tower before? A question mark punctuates the still air, my voice reverberates, his tiny face rocks back and forth with excitement. No, I say. It's my first time in Italy. I tell him to look at a carving on the side of the palace at 8:59 am.

In truth, I have become the monastery walls I've always wanted to live between, the order I called at eighteen and begged to join, to live within a vow of silence and a beautiful, purposeful habit.

Helen is given to fancies of religious experience, medieval frames locked away, self-imposed lashes, visions that trust the truth, isolation as a conduit for Art. She adores candle flames at night, wants to visit anchorite cells in pilgrimage, place her foot down near bars of a cell where Julian of Norwich, aching and inward, wrote varieties of holy love. She wants to conjure prose next to walls that compel her own quill pen. Instead, she stands at Saint Mark's Square near Marieke, feels herself a holy miracle born of short red hair and brown leather.

The bronze men atop the clock tower have yet to strike, the voice of our temporary tour guide points at church spires.

THE FIGURES BEFORE me are Adam and Eve, carved into the palace corner, stone grey punctuates the melancholy air. She points to him in accusation, his hand claims innocence. She is the power, he the long-winded speech. Between them, a small, timid, leafy stone tree vines up the building, two lower branches exactly as high as the genitals. Her breast, uncovered, glorious, her pubis reached to by a leafy hand, a single leaf obscures Adam's penis. The trees dictate the extent of their modesty as they stand witness, a Blakeian manifesto in solid grey stone.

I turn my head toward the clock tower just as two bronze statues pivot, lash out at the bell with fury. The chime seems unwilling, like cowering graven images motionless, hidden in the silent sensation that tomorrow will be the same as today.

It is 9:00. Already this tour has transposed me, even here from the edges of the days, I regard Eve's uncovered body. She unmolds herself, tells me to stay, she herself will take Marieke, carry her to a quiet hotel room, disregard blue shutters. I imagine me in her solid place at the corner of Doge's Palace and Saint Mark's Square, my hollow eyes regard tourists passing by, hope for a glimpse of blonde hair sweeping down a slender back.

Art itself has also taken my place here on the square. My hands again read Tintern Abbey for the first time on the park bench at the university. I lay on my stomach, knees curled, toes to the sky, the rain begins, tumbles down to meet black ink, I watch each drop fall on the words one by one.

Just now, the folds in a woman's dress remind me that Art has a consciousness, and that I had claimed myself a goddess just a few minutes prior. I peer down the colonnades and become an artist's cluttered room, I slumber between towers built two hundred years ago.

We enter the palace. My veins circulate through portraits, feel the breath of each intellect, wonder, fantasize about the large door handles, laughs heard in echo, ceilings thick with image. Marieke's shoulders look vaguely bored.

We walk the roped rooms, descend underground through a shrunken stairwell into the old prison cells under the palace. The barred windows at the Bridge of Sighs peer out over the canal. I take close-up pictures as if in a cage myself in the year 1750. The Bridge of Sighs, the bridge of sighs, I cannot say it enough times in my mouth. I want to sigh the bridge too and feel myself in utter misery. The tragedy of a stone bridge with a lovely name, beautiful suffering on a bench in the rain.

Inside Doge's Palace, my headset stops working properly. I hear scattered cracks in place of an imposter tour guide's voice, as irritating as her waist-length jacket. Her voice is scrawled walls, nosebleed voice in and out of the device, quiet then a clash of half-words that pierce the darkness I was just enjoying. It was not to be had for Helen, who calls herself goddess and breathes Italian air like Highsmith.

I remove the device entirely, hold it to my side. The room is astonished with quiet, tiptoe in the night quiet, train station gone empty after midnight. Silence marks the engravings on the sitting bench carved in Italian, words I cannot understand. A voice departs with a switch turned to off.

My mouth and the empty space in this large room

both hold languages they can no longer utter. I see one of many doors I am forbidden to open.

THE PALACE TOUR is over, Marieke is tired. I can see it in the way she scratches the side of her nose. She stands at the back of the crowd. I join her there. She had been commenting on the paintings for the benefit of high school girls who respond with aching eyes.

We leave the walls of the palace, stumble out into the clouded day, temperature a slight breeze across the forearm. Our snared-tooth tour guide says goodbye, have a lovely stay in Venice. How the mighty have fallen with her bandana and breathy skin.

Saint Mark's Square waits for us in the rain along with an angry nest of symmetrical columns. Someone in Italy's past swore out to the gods, and they answered with columns, each one a lash of whip, a fist, a tongue held solid. My red hair feels slightly damp, so I walk across the plaza to the cathedral. Its façade blends into the color of my black shirt. In response, I tiptoe around tiles woven into the cement ground.

The guard in front holds up his hand, it is Sunday

mass and we are excluded. The church belches us out into its No while my fingers trace marbled lines of the gold exterior. They have given me an archetype. Helen's desire must remain as accurate as this one shrill, metallic line. A gathering of clustered columns wraps its hands around my throat. We are to spend the afternoon in Venice on our own.

Richard at the bell tower stands erect with his hands in his pockets. Another tour mate for the week. He laughs at an unheard quip, rolls a map between his teeth, speaks with a British accent straight from Hyacinth's mouth. Richard the jovial, Richard the old, Richard the round, Richard the hand in pocket, Richard who makes Helen laugh, a smile creeps out from under her jaded lips as he recounts his favorite phallic symbols at Pompeii. Ostentatious in delivery, he translates Italian shop signs into Latin. He stands tall like the tower, bricked and sturdy, aligned with a stampede of stars that rain down on Helen's head when the lights go dim.

Some members of this dilapidated tour group are paying eight Euros to climb steps to the top of the bell tower, to gape over the edge, to get a slightly more expensive look at the water below. I will not do it. The once in a lifetime garbled cliché is synonymous with too many stairs. Misery. Richard agrees. We stand in wait along the plaza. When they all descend, we look at pictures they took of the view, reminders of our inarticulate refusal to climb stairs.

The bricks of the tower are perfect in their nonchalance and lack of empathy. Each brick the same color as the next, an unnatural turn.

This city, its dirt laden cellars and stench of polluted rivers, give the gondoliers a certain charm. Richard offers grandiloquence regarding the chemical composition of water under the bridge. It's ninety percent oil slick and ten percent piss, he says. It's the piss of a thousand Venetian drunkards who couldn't find their way home. I think the water must be medieval, buckets of piss and shit marauding over the edges of broken balconies, at long last arriving here to meet me, just below my feet.

In order to feel a sense of purpose for the day, I set out to buy a leather coin purse. Along the way, street names disappear, corner placards haunt me with their chipped paint and half-lettered sighs. I walk along canal banks, over carved bridges, try to read street signs so the geography under my feet will take shape into words. Geography in words, landscaped letters in a sound. A foreign tongue is also a foreign moment, thin avenues rested under clouds of a dream world. Tiny shops line streets like lemonade stands and arrive fully formed in the corner of my eye. Across an ornamented bridge, a small girl in sandals stands with her mother.

I enter an ancient bookstore that also sells hand-crafted quill pens, volumes in leather redolent of a nun's shawl. Strolling to prayer in a holy place, my fingers trace wicked words on book spines. Denuded, quiet letters carry sound but no texture, calm, peace, silence, a language I do not understand. The words go quiet here. They settle their anxieties, put away their revolvers, leave me to joy in their company, mild, dormant across the dinner table.

The day goes black and white in a bookstore. Helen becomes the shades of gray in a noir fantasy, dark rumors that obscure the eye and mouth, dogged corners laced in passion and poison that melt into the languid frames of an architect's pen. I am in a movie by Visconti, feet move between breaths the heroine heaves out over staircases.

I turn my head sharply. A whistling sound around the corner seems like it's for me, sudden intrigue, then immediate injustice as everyone's eyes wait for a suspended dramatic pause.

I paint myself into an Italian noir, try to disappear into the darkened façade. I realize these books divert me from my purpose. I return into the street with abandon.

Allow me off camera for a moment while I peer into the window of a gluttony. The scene: four young women, bare feet suspended in blue water. Tiny miracle fish suck at their flesh to soften the skin. They laugh one at a time. Murderous, miraculous event. I try to remain in black and white even while blue and red roar from off stage.

Pictures here are of glossed advertisements for peach cream, lotions to remove all traces of age.

The world is a sullen rooftop Helen wants to live under, seen for a moment through peat smoke and thick glass, lit by candles from four hundred years ago.

I see a burnt orange leather purse on a sturdy silver

loop next to the glass shop, blown glass too erudite for my taste. I need a new pocketbook, one not tattered, one not gasping its ravenous appetite for keys, coins all falling into the impossible spaces under the lining. The purchase is momentous, a feat of will and symbolic retribution. It's as daunting as a word scribbled off the page, as fireflies at the end of summer, as Picasso's blue paintings and Pollock's lonely rancor. How can one choose how to spend twelve Euros? Twelve Euros! An extravagance. No utilitarian argument could convince Helen that twelve Euros would not cause immediate penury.

Questions oppress the buying experience. Turquoise? Navy? Orange like autumn? Mauve like candy? Which shade of green? Three pockets or two? Zip or snap? Large or small? Leather or cloth? Long strap or short?

Handbags hang like unwilling enemies, each one a plight, an arm-gripped exhortation. I am about to simply surrender. Does anyone really need a handbag?

I decide to give it one more try, see if I can push through to the other side of owning. The eyes will decide. I hold a bright orange three-zippered shoulder bag in my hand, imagine myself walking down the street holding a cigarette, handbag in the picture. Is the handbag in the picture? Can I see it? I must admit it's not there. It's not right. No. On to the next. Purple? No. Black? No, certainly not. We mustn't give off too depressive an air. Not now. Not when Marieke may be just around the corner.

It's impossible. The rationale of inaction is the terror of green leather or brown. My mouth becomes dry, weight distributes along my feet.

I see Richard across the lane, ne-er do well grin across the lane. I shout out, Richard! Come here, new friend! I need help. Which color do you prefer? Tell me and I will proceed without question.

He says, Get the yellow one. The yellow one. Of course! Burnt yellow, on its way to orange. I leave the shop with an orange handbag and head toward Gallerie dell'Accademia.

A few people in the group want to go to the Accademia to see Da Vinci's Vetruvian Man. Marieke, dutiful in her long blonde hair and short black skirt, waits for us in the tourist shop center right next to a set of shaded benches. The sun has come out. Venice is warm, so I remove my jacket. Marieke will with luck notice the skin of my arms, though freckled.

We sit on benches out of the hot sun, old stone under our bodies as we tell of our purchases. She bought a gift for her parents. I bought a leather handbag for twelve Euros.

Richard eats an apple from a nearby stand. We wait for the younger girls who want to ride a gondola to the Accademia. Marieke will guide them there. I say I will take their picture, a moment of kindness shaken out of me by Marieke's teeth as she grins in my direction. She wants me to take a picture of the girls, so I do. I will take a thousand pictures, each girl will be smiling large and their mouths will be open in merriment. I will catch Marieke's silhouette in the background, she won't be able to steal her shadow back from me.

The girls board the gondolier. Marieke's plan is to walk, to meet them at the Accademia. Richard and I join her. It is the three of us, we relate jovialities, disparage tourist shops, praise bookstores along the way. Marieke's earrings brush against the top of her neck as I hold my arms to my side. She has removed her long green sweater so I can see the depth of her upper arms. The Bridge of the Accademia calls to us just ahead in the sun.

Marieke arrests me from three steps up, says to me, Stop here, You must take a picture of the most beautiful view in Venice.

The picture appears with polite gusto, just where the Grand Canal curves in toward the city. The view is a turn of her voice traveling out over three steps on a bridge, toward me exactly, the view is a lift to my arms in her direction where the camera meets the landscape. She has given me an order to create, her command results in an image. Footsteps across the bridge have drawn me into a version of beauty.

This time will not be the last, her voice will travel toward mine often as she relates stories of artists in love or recounts the history of a cathedral. From this moment, she speaks only to me. A direct command willed it, offering me this view of the canal banks. She has become the medium, the painted canvas that houses mystery and a grand imagination.

NOTHING IN THE Accademia will compare with the thinness of Marieke's fingers. The bend of her knuckles as she readjusts her dingy white tote.

We emerge into the plaza just in front of the museum, set a time to reconvene, then make our way alone into the building. My hopes are high for this first Italian museum. Others had been overjoyed at the thought of seeing Vetruvian Man, but I do not particularly care. Instead, I want romance, medieval portraits full of absence, triptychs of symbolic import, goddesses nude and men's bodies flayed alive by satyrs. Vetruvian Man is none of these. It's the clichéd chatter in pretend conversations with those who drive big cars with no remorse. Useless act, conversing, pinprick to cushion, a sop of bad succotash.

I think to myself, succotash is a crystalline word.

A small victory. Vetruvian Man is not on display this time of year. My satisfaction boils over their whined disappointment. Two women from Texas commiserate in the corner, complain that there should have been advance notification of the display schedule, consider asking for their money back. Their money back! They should be chained together and thrown to the bottom of the deepest canal in Venice, they do not deserve to breathe the same air as that muted portrait, just there, which looks down on them with a mocking smirk and a finger pointed to the sky. The painted man rains down on them my satiric smile. These two should be nailed to the wall, alive and wriggling, eyes forced open to stare at the blank space reserved for Vetruvian Man. Or, perhaps I am in error, perhaps they need a more ghastly ring of hell which only Dante could describe.

The steps are dark, the walls are dark, my feet at times don't know where to stand. The museum feels like a sunken hole dropped down into a furnace. The interior unsightly, and on edge. Richard and I wander the rooms getting lost and then finding ourselves yet again before the gigantic image of the last supper. I want the apostles to be eating each other in large godless growls to approximate the lack of color on the museum walls.

One bright moment is found in a small hallway, almost missed, just a short walkway from one room to another. A Bacchanal scene hangs on the wall, replete with intended rape in the scene, a woman fleeing, a group of unconcerned revelers gathered around a feast, sheep grazing, deep red fruit on vines and in potted bowls, a lush garden scene alongside a temple. The chased woman looks back on the scene as she escapes into the temple, silken dress voluptuous in its folds and sashes.

Richard says he enjoys a good Bacchanalia. I say I agree one hundred percent, minus the ravaging of women against their will. He agrees, yes, of course.

We stand in quiet observation. After a moment of silence, I imagine the running woman telling me to meet her inside the temple. I do. I am there now, inside. She takes refuge in my embrace, her bulging breasts against my own. I see red lace at her chest, she will be safe here with me. I touch her pale skin, a hand to breast in solidarity, in sated desire, in flight from one Bacchanal to another.

I want to remain a moment longer with this painting, but it is time to meet Marieke.

THIS AFTERNOON, VENICE seems a lifeless lullaby, bored gondoliers slacked at their stations, patrons at the nearest restaurant sit outside with Orangina and nothing to say. We exit the museum and take our places on steps overlooking the Grand Canal. Across the water, many colors of open shutters and entryways pattern the canvas. There is very little sound, mostly the monotonous drone of motorboats as they modernize the water.

My hair is redder than the painted mural along the walkway, it's how I remark the strength of the dye while others search for gelato. Dead Venice like dead Helen. Fingers along the way try to touch at the center of carefully hidden nerves. After walking for twenty minutes, we end up back at Saint Mark's, it is nearing twilight.

Helen is spared nothing, even on an evening full of shadows and geometry.

I use the light to detract from my worn face. The light is soft yellow resting on the length of the Square, long thick lines of dark shade cut across the long plaza to penetrate the feet of passersby. Shadows kneel down in the cemetery, ride out the waves, batter the edge of the island, long shadows cut us all into two and three and four as we amble about with shopping bags, shadows drown out angry columns and bring lovers together, cling desperate to the brick of the bell tower, dwarf the tower in size with their long necks and large appetites, shadows form new shadows in corners and in the crevices between fingers, shadows outside entwined fingers stroll two by two among the deep blue tiles that seem to define the ground.

It's all too much for one named Helen who notices Marieke's fake laugh near a woman from Texas. I decide, it is time for Helen to act the artist, follow her command to take a photograph. I will become photographer for the evening, imprison these shadows within the four walls of my camera lens. They will never escape. They will never even try. They will be as captured as the scratching sound of my pencil, will reside in the space between the falling light and Marieke's outstretched hand.

I remove my camera from my handbag. A group of hungry pigeons populate the plaza and I steal the remaining light from them. Two lovers about to kiss are clipped in two by an extended mass of obscured light.

They are nothing compared to the image I take of them. The blackened silhouettes of held hands, two parents with one child between them, I don't care for their bodies only for the dark outline that trails behind them. Image becomes absence of body, of solid mass, a busy camera pulling in the darkness.

No, Marieke, you were wrong when you spoke on the bridge. Here now, this glimpse of light on the side of the Bell Tower where you are sitting, that is the most beautiful view in Venice. Just stay there a moment, don't move, you mustn't move an inch of your arm or leg. Murder each disobedient muscle for my sake. Sit on a ledge along the tower, allow the sun to reach out its hand to your cheek, rest in a faded lively thin soft curl of shadow.

I take a photo while she looks away, and then I take another. Marieke's cheek meets the play of my camera lens. Dozens of shadows surround her stockinged feet before she moves, steps down, smiles in my direction.

I tell her the light is unbearable, unbearably beautiful, the haunted yellow across the blank plaza. She says in a quiet voice, "We have an artist here among us." The others look away in sublime disinterest. No, I almost say, don't share this moment with them.

She tells me to sit where she was sitting, it's her turn to take the picture. She says, You're the visitor after all, you should have your picture taken. I say Alright with heavy steps. I sit on the ledge where she had just been, attempt to look beautiful. My hair is too short, her hair is long. My legs too round while hers are thin. My jacket is black, hers green. I have tatters, she has lovely faded freckles.

The opposite of beauty is the opposite of Marieke, yet I am her model now. She shutters a few images, smiles, says they're not as good as mine. Seeing them I see a misshapen body, troll on a stump, malformed and monstrous with tight blue jeans and a large, black coat. The evening is a holy relic, consumed by the sun as it bends down across the earth, emblematic of a command and a surreptitious photograph, a bell tower at dusk and a woman's face obscured.

Marieke at the tower, the woman running from Bacchus. Marieke and the holes in my pocket. Marieke and the bookshelf I will place her on. Shadows that fall on a body in the middle of the blackest night.

I SEND A picture home to Marcel to relate the evening, tell him I have a crush on the tour guide. He tells me That's fantastic with an exclamation point. He sends a note that the boys are doing well, they are learning how to make their own short films after school each day. I offer enthusiasm in return, which is genuine but out of place.

I look around and remember that Marieke has gone to check the restaurant for tonight's dinner. We wait, loiter around the bell tower. Richard suggests we have a coffee in the café across the way. No reason to decline. I am adrift in shadows, cold film of water still lacing my raincoat. It is cold. Coffee. Yes.

The café cannot hold more than a few people. We make our way past barstools single file, adjust ourselves at the counter, no room even to move stools from their places to sit. Two others from the tour join us, stand single file and try to order coffee in Italian.

Café? Grazie. The barista speaks to us in English. A small sip, a splintered bitter mouth, my American palate. Richard flirts with the woman behind the counter, slim and noticeably Italian, while I surrender to my need to use the restroom. I have suffered the indignity for several hours already.

The restroom is coveted, tucked into a slight corner. The door opens outward, awkward, so far out it almost touches patrons at the counter. One must breathe out a Scusami to others drinking coffee to politely exit the toilet.

I make my way over, try to blend into the dark wooded walls, coffee thick in my throat. The door is locked, of course. Poor Helen. Where to stand to wait? Here, where my body blocks the door? There, to excuse myself all over again? Dire circumstances! My head is a tangle of uprooted vines wrapped around my aching feet.

After just a moment, the door opens with my arm in its way. A blue-eyed petite woman makes her way out of the small room, slides her body against mine fully to find her way out. Our eyes and breasts meet outside the bathroom door. She smiles, tells me in accented English,

There is no more toilet paper. I say, That's okay. She says, You'll need toilet paper.

Helen, what to do after your breasts have just touched hers? Resign to no toilet paper? She'll think only of your piss stench! Ask the Italian barista for toilet paper? It's not even a question.

The blue-eyed petite woman shouts to the barista, This woman needs toilet paper!

I see her eye wink at me while I stand in glum dispirit with a Thank you on my lips.

The barista: It's in the cabinet right behind you. Helen thinks: Right behind me? Again what to do? Open the cabinet, pull out a roll of toilet paper in front of all these people? It can't be.

The heat from my cheeks penetrates the café. Just now, I wish myself a nun deposited safely within Saint Mark's cathedral. Before I can act, the woman opens the cabinet, places the roll of paper in the restroom on my behalf, says It's all yours. All mine? Her breasts have risen to the corner of my embarrassment. All mine. I step toward the small toilet.

MY FEET BURN in these wet socks, the damp ground feels ponderous and pretend. I walk alone on a brazen side street, sodden grey hides its colors. The evening is full of contradictions. I navigate bold stone walkways, feel the leather of my new purse, enter a corner bookstore cramped with swollen Italian prose. The words are deliciously impenetrable.

A couple beside me search for a phrasebook which causes me irritation. I am irate until I overhear them ask for conversational Greek.

I wonder if there's a difference between murder and Art, if one could set the two on each side of an algebraic equation. I decide to logic it through over dinner.

The bookstore becomes a bore with empty bodies turning pages. Volumes overwhelm my evolving anger at the phrasebook couple.

I leave, drift back to the plaza steps, see newly familiar faces after a day on the town in Venice. I wonder if this tour will end the way I imagine. Marcel had told me, You should go on a trip, somewhere you'll feel among the ancient. I had said, Yes, you are likely correct. Now I am here in the footsteps of Marieke. I sit on a step in the cold, suggest to myself that I take her home with me, or at the hotel tonight, watch her turn channels of Italian TV.

Day Three
Ravenna

THE EARLY MORNING hotel staff helps us toward Ravenna with cups of coffee and damp croissants. The streets slack-jawed and hollow, the wait for the bus indeterminate, our early eyelids complement the heavy Venetian mist. Each long minute here on the darkened sidewalk renders our coffee cups unwilling wardens as we demand in our quiet ways a proper breakfast. Even the Texans stand in wait with suitcases propped against their legs.

The wait goes five minutes, ten, accentuates our sunken eyes. Today is day three, tomorrow the halfway point. I breathe in the lifeless silent morning. I comfort myself with a glance toward Marieke's sleepy eyes just as the bus arrives.

The pastry entirely unsatisfying, the coffee just warm

enough to settle aching arms, I nestle into a plush oversized seat and use my raincoat as a pillow. After a few tiny street corner turns, the bus begins to drone along the highway toward Ravenna, the location of Dante's tomb, after which we will board the bus again to arrive in Florence for dinner.

I regard the Italian landscape, search for the arrival of full dawn, come to understand the camera lens from Italian cinema. The colors, golden streams of patched earth, solid yellow, bare hints of green. A sepia landscape names the countryside here and draws the sleep from me.

The roads of Northern Italy doze as the sun slowly rises. My eyes open from time to time at the sound of a Texan cackle, they meet its energy for a moment, then allow the yellow fields to lull me back into sleep.

I doze, I wake, I check the time, write a few words in a notebook, bits of poetry remembered badly from grand anthologies, jot a few notes about the previous day. I had been determined not to forget a moment of the trip, but now it all seems a dusty leather briefcase opened and empty.

We ride along for hours to get to Ravenna. I think about Marcel along the way. He is home just now, likely reading to the children or telling them a mildly horrific story from Poe or Lovecraft that will scare them immensely as they try to fall asleep. These stories, he says, will give them their own horrors, safe ones in our warm little house, necessary preparation for their futures as artists.

I remember when Marcel and I first met at a part-time retail job we both worked. He convinced me to read David Mamet, ignored me in favor of editing a novel when there were no customers. His early work explores criminal depravity, as a result I spent much of my twenties desiring the depraved. Desiring to touch a woman's neck in secret, to empty my pockets of murder, to feel the taste of two dollars stolen from a retail till when the manager wasn't looking.

His novels made it seem so easy, giving in to temptation, imagining the next scene on the stage, placing oneself outside the paranoia that comes with being sought. His use of the alphabet mimics a desire for wrath, a sullen handshake, the man on the train who steals your wallet, a child's glance and the deal they make to stab you with a fork at the dinner table.

I desire the unconscious to tell me what to do next. Shrill voices clatter down the highway, create notions of harm on my fingertips. There must be a way to block out the noise. Would I even have a few words to say to the mouths of these women?

Helen's sheer anxiety is the absence of words in a crisis. Her self-awareness just now comes from never having tugged at a woman's scarf. Two women, two scarves. One pulled to shut a mouth, the other to draw a mouth closer.

Highsmith glances at me from the seat adjacent. I dig in my bag, find the novel, read a few lines.

My eyes give up in sleep. I doze almost until we reach Ravenna. As my mind drifts, I wonder if there is any way to make a university professor the subject of intrigue without a knife hidden in the drawer of her office desk, leather-bound tomes piled all around. I consider the chickens on the set of *Cul-de-Sac*.

WE STEP OFF the bus, the day is full of sleep. We all lunge down heavy toward a heavy lane of foot traffic just next to where the bus will park and wait. I consider all the ways this town looks like any other, cars an endless parade of smoke, high heels on sidewalks, suddenly become unnerved at the sight of construction cranes in a foreign city. Too familiar. Or am I unnerved that I am unnerved?

The small side street takes us to a tunnel that stretches under the main highway. It's lined with extravagant graffiti, colors splashed across face and body into their singing slogans and painted figures that look to be vaguely political. Tiny anarchies of underground resistance. The colors pierce the mid-morning gloom and draw me into Ravenna's main square. My hands have rested firmly in my coat pockets.

The Square has been plunged into yellow and I have been dragged along with it. Paint chips and potted flowers line its four sides while casual diners eat brunch down the street. My feet hardly know how to escape the cracks in the wall seeped with hundreds of years of rainfall.

The square is vast and nearly empty. I hear the hissing sound of Texans deciding next where they will eat and the grunts of Richard as he clears his morning throat. The plaza becomes an aching cigarette. It waits to be brought to life in a movie star's lips. It longs for rapid heartbeat, bated breath, magnificently bored, quiet in respect for its own age.

I stand in a small circle with my tour mates, listen to the mumble and chirp of words. The ledge flowers look lonely in the light. I regard the others, realize I am the only one who could appreciate the observation. I hear the word gelato again in the vicinity of questions about the location of the nearest ATM machine.

Marieke stands in the center of the square, magnifying its cavernous features. Her presence fills the square, dims the garbled voices looking for food. She holds a folded city map in her hands, knit-browed and contemplative. I want to step up from behind her, look over her shoulder and say Can I help? just to get closer to her earrings and to explore the fragrance in her hair. I notice my eyes resting on her thin frame while others in the circle look in my direction. I must stay careful not to allow the eyes to remain too long, I must stay in this average length of circle rather than take one step closer to her now.

The square goes quiet, empty except for her as I listen for sounds of a folded paper map. She wears light denim pants and white tennis shoes without socks so I can see her ankles and the length of her legs. One of the Texans exhales the word Dante and her breath takes the shape of a tomb.

The lunch we eat at a small side restaurant sickens me slightly. A slick slab of mozzarella on two pieces of stale bread. Normally, such a lunch would suit my palate perfectly, but something about the weeks-old quality of the products made my stomach queasy and my hands begin to sweat.

After lunch, the Basilica calls to us in the form of Marieke's long stride. Again, we follow, green sweater blazing ahead. She consults the map like it's a form of religion.

The Basilica, they say, is famous for its mosaic tiles. I must admit I am a skeptic, more aesthetically interesting are frescoes cracked and faded along barren streets and inside dusty refurbished churches. The patience required for the mosaic arts are a source of consternation for me. Creation comes to a full-throated stop in recalcitrant shards of glass.

Standing outside the Basilica, I am struck by incongruity, a long thick ancient façade and a grease-laden luxury car, simultaneous along the grey walkway. I look to the sky for assistance. It only desires obscurity, so I amble in through the doorway to see what other silences await. A grimed water fountain sustains the greeting, it has stationed itself by the door along with antiquated paper cups, a tiny gem in this old place. Inside is dark, and deep, the main city square disappears. This place should be the center. Instead, it is an oversight, a petulant end to the path that starts in a graffiti-laden tunnel.

The mosaics impress me less than the way groups of bodies form in solid mass around the wishing fountain, perhaps originally part of the church, but now repurposed to gain a few extra tourist Euros a day. Helen the cynic. That is, until she steps under the arched doorway, feels herself compelled by tiny shades of glass set in meticulous order to form scenes from Biblical mythology. The rapture of glass in a wall, miracle and crime, a swollen afternoon thick with thievery, a forlorn candle-lit evening spent writing words on a page no one will read.

No street corner shops here, only the brittle formula that holds these pieces together. Tight and grasping, they cling to the walls and ceiling, they find their places in an order designed by the skin of a human hand.

I STAND IN the center of the dome in contemplation of the fingertips that must have touched each small miracle of color. Just then, I feel a hand rest lightly at my shoulder blade. A hand to shoulder, a nighttime game, a hand to shoulder, turned book page, a hand, a cigarette lighter, a hand, my glasses fallen and broken, a hand, a letter sent through the mail without a name, a hand, a stolen suitcase, a window left open in the rain, a hand, every scene in a novel by Highsmith. She has laced her hand on Helen's shoulder and has asked with nonchalance how she likes the mosaics.

How do I like the mosaics?

Mosaics are what I want to say. The mosaics. Yes,

how do I? Think of something clever to say Helen with a hand not brushing but resting on your light blue shirt worn today instead of black. Perhaps the new color has worked. Her hand after all is on blue, and not black. One hand, one invitation too many. One hand may as well be a door opened to the black of night or the blue in the wall of the bookstore.

I say, They are beautiful, difficult to imagine, the labor, the artistic vision, the patience, the care of each hand.

The artistic inspiration of a hand under mosaic tiles will become the peering eye through the window of a tour bus, the well-situated body set to receive the knuckled bend of finger, the lips her hand requests. I wonder if Marieke imagines the placement innocuous, she must in the nerves of her hand which now have penetrated my flesh in its fingertips.

I have said enough. You have said enough Helen.

Wait. Marieke's hand on my shoulder. It cannot mean the same as her hand on the Texan's body, can it? She has given me an indication here, I must take it. She is telling me how unlike an overcooked teacher of high school English I am, how little I speak about art as if it were viciously branded cattle at a rodeo. Neither am I jovial good-natured Richard. I am not a bored adolescent thick with satire. I am none of these people she has also touched. There must be only one conclusion. She has decided to be bold in Marieke's way, a boldness welcome under the blue and gold ceiling, a welcome brashness she will only enjoy more from this point forward. She has reserved her touch for me, singular and in solitude. She has reserved a touch for Helen to say I am not touching another just now. It is only you who feel the weight of my hand and hear my breath alongside your cheek.

The hand departs. Marieke departs. She is on to another tour patron to earn her two-hundred-dollar tip. Most important to note is whether she touches anyone else as she makes the rounds.

She approaches the larger stomached man who has been a source of disquiet for the last two days. Her fingers do not touch his sweated yellow shirt. No, she will not reach out to feel his body and heavy breath. They talk. I can only half hear what they say. I hear nothing about artistic vision or the hands that shaped it. That remark was unique to me, she will remember me for it as she suffers the company of these goblins. They become more gruesome by the day. One would never know based on Marieke's smile though. She is very good at her job, performs it with an eager appeal, she appraises each gnarled smile to make it feel adequately interesting.

I remark under my breath, There shall soon be no need to pretend a smile. But then I remember that she already knows. She told me with the palm of her hand.

The dark church is darker as Marieke takes steps away, greets others, touches no one. The absence of hand tells me as much as the heat still clung to my blue shirt in the shape of thin fingers. Yes, it has been confirmed. The pennies at the bottom of the fountain have confirmed it, too.

Helen is given to another fit of image, another bend to Marieke's command. I will capture in image the incipience of crime, the beginning of voyeuristic charade, the inching closer of my hand to hers at a dinner table or over lunch. I will begin to insist on answers to questions about her parents, her university, her friends who live in Rome. An ostensible set of tourist questions. Yes, the beginning needs a ceremony, a baptism, a holy communion, a solemn celebration of this space which has brought it to turn. Here, walls. Here, water. Here, the images she saw as her flesh made contact with mine, purposefully and without measure, the bend of wall saw it happen and turned a shade of pink.

I SAY TO myself that Helen must take photographs now, images of such aesthetic beauty that Marieke will desire to touch them in her hands. Photographer Helen comes to life, brings her cauldron of witches brew to work as magic, captures with a cunning eye the colors just before they change through the stained glass window, images of Christ and young Mary. Thousands of images scatter off light as the penny fountain takes its shape, as feet bite the stairs in long bellows stepping outside into the sun, images of glistening gold tiles as they meet the red ones underneath, the cracks hidden, the design invincible, images of blue green water rest in peace on the ground near a small pool of stained shadow, punctured, checkered water. Rays of light reflected from a pool carry the shadow of Jesus while the sun is out, and then goes black at night. A crack in the grey stone walkway reveals the shadows underneath us too, reveals hesitant feet below fingers lifted to mouth in contemplation, a casual cast of light along a handrail worn smooth over many years, the red of one single tile extracted from all the rest to give it a singular purpose at the end of my camera lens. The turned face of a young girl mirrors the windows behind her, the loose end of Marieke's curl bounds down the small of her back, the long lonely face of a church guard waits with folded hands for five o'clock, angled yellow villainous light peers in triangle upon a door kept mostly closed near the faded blue pallor of a worn cement floor.

The manic images eventually subside, the camera is the failure of my artistic eye. Discouraged with the outcome of my labor, I realize none of these images would be a fitting end to the moment.

I stumble over a step as I leave the church, take my place on the ledge outside the door. The architecture lifts its own symbolic features, each layer of stone and brick a new dimension. Arches climb the sky like a revelry. The bricks take pride here, lines on a printed page could not compare to the angles of these square stones, each step up to the balcony mourns its view out over the freeway.

Helen is alive with geometry, with textured layers of the artist's drafting table. If only I were a painter, I could exhale the color my eyes turn when Marieke takes her place on the ledge right next to me.

I say to her, I was just admiring the peculiar architecture as it appears on the side of the church, you see, the architecture climbs the sky.

She says she's always loved the way she gets lost in the stonework here, feels at peace surrounded by the calming shades of yellow. The landscape is one with the old buildings here, she says. I've always wanted to take a course in Italian architecture, but never had the time, she says.

I tell her, we are learning all we need to know, just here, right now, in our shared appreciation.

She smiles, and then a Texan calls her name. Her head turns from me. I have lost her next to a blackbird throating its bellow out onto the green grass next to the ledge. The Texan squeals her desire to see the tomb of Dante, which is several blocks away.

MARIEKE TRACES THE route along the map on tiptoe, takes our footsteps along alleyways getting us all lost and then found again. She handles herself with deftness no matter the circumstance. Even a lost tour group on its way to Dante's tomb can't trip her up. I was impressed and I told her so along the way.

Dante rests at Rue Alighieri. The woman who wanted to see Dante makes it known all around, a toadstool squeal issues forth as she sees the corner placard. I recall a student of mine who once wrote "I stood on the corner of silence and Alighieri." I think perhaps the young man was not so creative after all.

This woman shrinks my bones down to size, sounds like an unintended slap of wet shoe on a freshly waxed floor, the sound of claws tearing up carpet, or a high school drama queen who thinks she knows how to sing.

We stand on the corner and listen to dutiful fingers fly over camera clicks, expressions of profound affectation.

Who here has actually read Dante? I cannot believe such gnarled fingers could ever have turned his pages. At this point I doubt even Marieke has read *The Inferno*. Certainly, none here would understand Eliot's invocation.

Expressionless eyes look upon the hollow grave, blind stares, inscriptions in Italian and the carved velvet of Dante sitting in a chair. The white sepulcher seems out of place shoved in a lonely corner, given to fits of solitude despite tourists all around. Dante ends up entombed in sport, though not in body, on a dusty street corner in the town where Marieke touched my shoulder. My feet begin to tire.

The Texan woman weeps on the street corner. Her overwhelmed mouth issues out muffled sobs as she wipes her face with her sweater. She teaches Dante, she informs us all, and here she is at his resting place. Her sobs dampen the morning. Marieke places her hand around the woman's shoulders for comfort and a listening ear.

Marieke, don't be foolish. This woman knows nothing of Dante, his obsession with Beatrice who stilted him and for whom he wrote and died, nothing of the lengths obsession will go when the obsessed is handy with a quill pen, nothing of the way young Dante must have looked deep into his own sunken eyes when Beatrice said No, you will not do, and nothing of his rungs of Hell that show her within what depths he sees her.

This woman and her tears reveal Marieke's weakness. If she truly knows of Dante she'd be standing here to the side of the street with me, vaguely mocking a woman's handkerchief and heartfelt response, looking forward to the next set of windowed landscapes on the way to Florence.

The sobs eventually cease, we drag ourselves back to the coach. Marieke tells us all how wonderful it was to see someone so moved by a part of the tour. The Texan smiles at her good fortune while I sink lower into my seat and reach for an empty notebook.

THE HOTEL EXTERIOR in Florence is decorated in cat's tongue pink, accented deep blue along the small frames of wall and sill. We arrive late in the afternoon, after a day of sun seeping in through windows of the coach and warming us to sleep. Marieke had taken off her long, oversized scarf as she played guessing games with some of the passengers. I saw it all, how she turned her head slight and downward, how she laughed at someone's attempt at wit. I saw the scarf come down from the neck and placed onto the seat, saw the frail red lace at the trim of her shirt, saw the way her hand rested for a long time on the back of the seat two rows up from me. She must have held her hand there so I could see the connection between us, to tell me she is there with me while she turns over cards in a game she invented to play with strangers.

As we leave the bus to enter the hotel, I tell her she must show me that game someday. She attempts to explain the rules, but we are interrupted by the sound of suitcases in someone else's hand.

The hotel is larger than it should be, sheltered by a large gravel courtyard in front where we unload our bags and try to make peace with fate. Half the hotel is under construction, great boarded windows and scrap metal piles in corner shadows on the ground outside. The gravel under our feet echoes the street cars as they disappear.

A large room key, straight out of an old Italian noir film, is placed into my hand, just the invitation I need to front-door-locked fantasies and arms spread wide in relaxation. My first-floor room is just down the hall from the hotel entrance, around the corner is a large sitting room with couches, side tables, travel brochures, and an unattended coffee bar.

I stay in my room for thirty minutes before I am ready to join the crowd. This room, a time-woven artwork of dilapidation and class. I admire the worn carpet and promiscuous chandelier, unconcerned holes in the wall and gold-plated water faucets. A fanatical blend of care and discard that flatters every hotel room fascination. This room, just to the side of a roped hallway of grey cement and paint chips means there are no neighbors to offend my sleep, no noise to draw me from reverie, only surreptitious bodies coming around the corner. A perfect room. A perfect evening.

Marieke will soon draw us out into the moonlit streets.

I wait for her in the sitting room, a silent bore, at first.

I enter with nothing to lose and my leather purse around my shoulder, the space silent and empty, like a living darkness, lantern lit and solemn. There are meant to be many voices here, enjoying drinks, settling in for long conversation surrounded by deep pink curtains. But here there are no voices, only the deep sound of Helen's breath as she lets out a late afternoon sigh.

How can I steal this empty feeling from the place I am sitting? Emptiness like Art without an audience, pure, exact, undistracted, firm to its purpose. Helen feels alone in a large room, the silence not even subdued by a single distant noise, the silence impossible, apocalyptic.

I see a picture on the wall, one half Botticelli's Venus, the other half Michelangelo's David. One set of vacant eyes, one set full of lust. These two are with me here in the silent sitting room.

I find myself submerged in a large, soft-cushioned chair. I place my foot on the ottoman, arrange my purse and jacket beside me. Innocuous landscapes line the walls, cozy English cottages as respite from the mono-chrome yellow of Italy. Bright flowers, tiny white houses, grand green mountains lush with picturesque waterfalls and sheep grazing. These are not Italian memories.

My eyes rest back on David. I try to feel impressed, but the picture is small and the face makes little sense. At least Venus has a breast to admire, her long red hair reminds me to touch my own, recently shaved but growing. The image is cropped so she appears only to her waist, the other extravagance left for tomorrow. Some days, the truth is everywhere.

I wonder vaguely where the others are, but then remember it's almost thirty minutes before our scheduled time to meet. They all must be laboring over minutia in their rooms. Why am I not in mine?

I sit, wait, imagine my hands touching dusty volumes in the bookcase near the coffee bar. Boredom, lethargy. The sitting room swallows me down its gullet, leaves me alone in a dark belly, consumed first, then entitled, proprietary, my own dim lamplight, pen in my hand. The deep cushioned seat and stationary pens wait for letters to be written, stamped, and sent. The middle of an appetite, den of envy, slow descent into deeper darkness that will end with a breaking of chains. The silent sitting room has told me its secrets, and they are visions, ones I will attempt to recreate, vacancy and lust sink deeper into quiet, each cross over with a smile.

Helen alone in a quiet room ends with inner monologue marked by despair. She bellows to no one philosophical objections to the color pink and to the way David's shoulders seem unapproachable. She is the sculpted and the sculptor, alone in a chair waiting for darkness to come, without light, without favor, without mallet in hand.

Helen, rooted firmly in the imagination, begins to doze in comfort and warmth. Perhaps the chair has become too inviting, perhaps it threatens her with just an ounce too much of the unconscious. Venus and David turn into simplistic clichés of fine art on an Italian hotel wall.

Perhaps I must walk, she thinks.

Yes, I will go see those volumes on the shelf that now seem so neglected, waiting there just for me.

MY FEET MEET the ground in a burst of bottled energy, feel like sludge all over the ground. The body heavy with age pulls itself from the chair, puts one foot out a step toward the far side of the room. Sound of pant thigh the only sound, the smile on my lips the only sound, my hand in my hair the only sound, a head turned sharply, the only sound. I turn my head to make sure no one is looking into the large glass windows or staring in from the veranda.

Now look this other way and see.

Resting solemn on a sofa cushion, one which I could not see before, the light blue pink grey white of Marieke's oversized scarf, which buried her neck all day, which her thin fingers adjusted and re-adjusted all day, and then removed in the sun along the route. Marieke's scarf and white tote, papers strewn almost out of the top, tour guide policies and procedures, attendance lists, room key numbers. Who knows really what could be written on those typed pages?

The scarf rests atop the bag, isolated, alone, quiet, inert. Marieke has done a disservice here, leaving her things in this empty room. Presumably, she is just down the hall taking care of tour business or accommodating a patron or speaking Italian with the hotel manager.

Presumably, she will return shortly to collect her things before taking us all out to dinner and wondering if she should sit next to me or make another woman happy.

Marieke's scarf taunts me with its pale colors and lack of emotion, taunts me with texture I've not felt, warmth I've not endured, the length of it reaches an unknown length along my willing body. Marieke has made the mistake, though unaware of her crime, of leaving an item of such import all alone with these pink walls. It is a crime, and Helen is the victim. The room victimized too by negligence and frayed edges.

The room is empty except for the presence of my hands, Marieke's scarf, and the memory of a neck bared, pulled close in theory on a bus line. My hands cannot bear the weight of memory.

Reach out, look around, reach out, look to the left and right, reach out, look to the window, reach out, look again, reach out my fingers until the scarf is in my hand and fumbled in quickly under my black raincoat hung along my arm. Leather handbag and black coat leather handbag black coat adorn my arms and that is all.

I make my way back thirty steps to my locked room

around the corner. I see hotel patrons at the front counter down the hall while I find the key in my pocket. The scarf, the long soft fabric under my coat, folded there along the skin of my arm, enters my room in silence just as it lay before. Spread on the bed in silence, folded neatly in silence, unfolded in silence, wrapped around a bare neck in silence, the only sound an attempt to wrap the fabric just so like Marieke. How exactly does she make it hold just so around her neck? Helen tries and fails in the mirror, tries again, fails again. Marieke's bright face and white teeth give this object life, now Helen's red hair gives it purpose.

IT IS ALMOST time to meet the rest of the group. Almost dusk, the hotel lobby waits for 6:00 when our feet will travel outside to a restaurant for dinner.

Folded neatly again, the scarf takes up residence at the bottom of my suitcase, wrapped in a worn plastic bag reserved for soiled clothes. A turn of the door knob, one confirmed lock, and I step out into the lively hallway now filled with hungry tour mates. I see Marieke waiting with a cold neck.

We leave the hotel behind, I in my jacket, she in her sweater. She had quietly asked the hotel attendant on the way out if anyone had turned in a scarf to the front desk. The No was monumental, it set me out the door in good humor. We followed her once again, carefully, down busy Florentine streets.

Night had come quickly, streets are dark when the sun goes down here. Sidewalks, a balancing act so inadequate for large American bodies, they labor to stay afloat as Marieke marches quickly to make our reservation time. All along these streets is so much to see, yet I cannot look around. I must pay careful attention to the placement of my feet, to each stretch of uneven cement, each unmeasured curb.

The traffic splits the group in two, Marieke hurries off ahead. I fall to the very back in solidarity with her. I think, do not worry, Marieke. I will follow everyone for you, I will make sure these young girls do not lose us in the city. She snakes and vines her way through side streets and miracles of modern architecture.

Every few moments I look up from the ground to see a new bookshop, books and books and books all along the path to the restaurant. The spines reach out to me, words surround my lunging body. Books and books. Books about travel and desire and ones by university scholars and about political intrigue, each shop vows the same shelf, each letter jumps into the street and avoids traffic to reach me. I do not stop. I leave them behind, the words, I can still hear them calling Helen, Helen, here is your old home, it smells of leather and dust, it all waits for you here, if you remain still, if you stop your feet from moving right now, look over here, the signs are fading, we are almost ready to close our gates, the signs will flash out soon if you don't hurry. Books, letters, foreign alphabets, they all come they go as my body keeps moving past, keeps one eye on Marieke and the other on the pavement. I am destined to fall over unless I look carefully at the ground. Yet the books are too numerous and frightening as they recede. They haunt me in images of dark lighting and a cat on my lap, they are the result of recycled dreams of days to read books without end. The stories that carry me into a bookshop in Florence are the ones I leave behind as I follow her long blonde hair.

The streets get smaller. The sidewalk fades.

We cross suddenly toward a darkened restaurant window.

THE RESTAURANT WALLS are all mirrors. Reflections trick the eye, angles cross each conversation, mirrored columns bear the weight of the ancient building. Even the booths are mirrored, patrons must watch themselves eat. The mirrors tell each place setting where it should rest, each fork to mouth a sign of infinity, the afterlife, each sip of wine a portal to eternity.

Richard and I sit at a small booth, jovial in mind. I smile and place my wit on the table. Richard matches in crude humor. Tour mates split up, sit in different parts of the restaurant, order their wine with question marks.

Each person in our group is given the same meal, a package deal, except for Marieke and me and one of the young girls, all delightfully vegetarian. I thank the gods for turning me against meat one year ago so I might have this solidarity with a bare neck in a mirrored restaurant. We three get salad, vegetable soup, a plate of cheese. The meat eaters receive an eerie turkey roll with yellowed mashed potatoes. The Italian idea of American cuisine is not far off. Richard looks toward me disgusted, I laugh aloud at his misfortune, and offer to share my salad. A roll of turkey is a thing of beauty, a decrepit reminder of the way we are all foreign. I look around while Richard tells me the history of Julius Caesar and describes the sights we will see of ancient Rome.

These mirrors fracture faces, fragment eyes and nose, smiles turn to horrors and human heads are brought up for sacrifice.

I search for a glimpse of Marieke but cannot find her. She must be seated at the one table not visible from here. I wonder if I could at least get a glimpse of her green sweater, just a corner, or perhaps I could catch sight of her blonde hair. I wonder if she left the restaurant. According to tour rules, she could be fired for such an infraction. No, she wouldn't have left us here. I decide she is purposefully hiding and that I don't care anyway. If she is hiding, I will turn my attention more fully to Richard's stories, perhaps glean an anecdote or two to inform the tour guides, to make me seem more intelligent, perhaps even interested in anything other than the medieval.

OVER DINNER RICHARD and I design a plan to resurrect the disabused coffee bar in the sitting room at the hotel. We'll ask the hotel desk person if we can make coffee there, use the supplies they seem to store in its cupboards, enjoy the sitting room over a cup of fresh evening coffee or tea.

We leave the restaurant with a light step, one long single file exhortation signals to the city that we are on the move with solid boots on the street side. We follow Marieke all the way back to the hotel. She stands on the gravel counting to make sure we have all arrived. I linger, stand toward the back of the crowd. I want to be counted last, to seem roundabout, as if I could breathe this air forever, a strategy to have a last word with Marieke.

She counts me, all here, she says with a show of teeth. I tell her about the coffee plan as we enter the hotel together. Say, would you like to join us? Richard is in full form tonight. He'll make us both laugh, and we can save that poor neglected coffee bar from ruin.

She hesitates, says she should get some sleep. I say, I understand. She says, then, with a turn of the head toward me and her fingertips raised to the height of her chest, You know, I think I will join you after all. It's still early, plenty of time for sleep. Just for a little while, yes. See if we can use that coffee bar and I'll meet you both there.

My arms rise to the height of hers. I breathe in as she turns to walk away.

Richard, I say, let's get this done. Marieke wants to join us.

We ask the hotel manager. He says, Of course, and the evening is complete in one hour. One hour in which Helen puts on her best show of gregarious energy, she moves the body feet to hands to mouth. One hour of attentiveness to Richard's jokes and irreverence, to Marieke's amusement over coffee. I make her coffee for her, place the cream and sugar to the side of the saucer with deliberate care, ask her if there is anything else she needs, Mademoiselle.

Eventually, she departs. Her legs appear younger than her face, her small white shoes youthful, a bounce step toward the stairs.

THE EVENING MIRACLES end, so I tread around the corner back to my room for the second time today. This time, I leave the sitting room with a different piece of Marieke. This time the memory of a cup placed to her lips behind a furled brow.

The night is dark outside, and I am tired. Fatigue in my hands and knees as I undress, replace one set of clothes with another set for night. My throat worn and old, my shirt hangs on my shoulders, slumped and slovenly. Mirrors won't do me any good here either, I think. Off to sleep in a few minutes. I enter the restroom for nightly ablutions, place my forehead close to the mirror, look into my own grey eyes. Blemishes everyone must have seen today revel in my lack of amusement.

I turn around, see for the first time a tile missing from the wall just above the toilet. An entire bathroom tile, at least two inches in area, is gone. Was it there before? Has it just been removed while we were out? Had I simply not noticed it before? It is entirely possible. But not probable. I peer down into the blank space behind the tile, see darkness stretching into the wall. No whites of eyes, no light. I think this must have been her doing, otherwise, how am I just now seeing such a thing? Someone could now be looking at my reflection, seeing my blemishes from their vantage point behind the wall. A set of ears could easily hear the sound of urination coming from the toilet below me. Someone could see all of that, you see, so how could this evening be mere happenstance? It's preposterous. Even more than the thought of a peering eye is the thought of a peering mind, the thought of someone able to look but deciding against it.

What to do about this hole in the bathroom wall, a source of humiliation and a hidden camera, the wide eyes of a private moment, or an investigator calling my name, telling me I am being rescued from a devastating fire before I can smell the smoke?

The visions become part of my reality with adept speed, so I decide I must close the gap all the way to the other side of the wall. I pick up a fine idea, a washcloth, folded, a white hotel washcloth folded into a bundle and placed with vigor just into the hole, push it in as far as it can go, farther to make sure no extra eyes can get through. Problem solved.

I decide not to tell Marcel the next day. I keep it for myself out of sheer romance. The delicious suspense of someone spying.

After the issue is resolved, I lay on the bed, eyes half open as I try to watch some television. Voices seem to shout and all I want is quiet, I want the words to calm down for the night.

I pick up Highsmith and click off the television, read a scene about a chance encounter in the lobby of a Venetian hotel. I think to send a message to Marcel. I hadn't communicated since yesterday, he may worry.

I send a brief note. I'm doing fine, fun day in Florence, falling asleep reading Highsmith. He'll appreciate the spontaneous alliteration.

Just as I receive a message back, the novel drops to my side with fatigue. There will be decisions to make tomorrow and I must get plenty of sleep to make them. I fall asleep with visions of thin sidewalks and moonlit streets and remember that tomorrow will be the day I am introduced to Michelangelo.

Day Four
Florence

BREAKFAST IS A menace, a snagged lazy day, a long slow progression. I take my small plate of fruit and toast to a table for four in the small dining room adjacent to the sitting room. The diners, flush with light already this morning, circle and betray the silence with their mockery of good conversation. They swear that their stories are the most amusing, shout the results of their evening libations, recount with alacrity and open throats the missteps and purchases from the day before.

I sit at a table alone in protest. The ribald lack of peace, boring such boring bores, wasting breath, bored voices astound my hands as I peel a hard-boiled egg and put it in my salted mouth. The day is given a sunny disposition when all I want are clouds, a glorious dark day. The assault on my mealtime peace is complete when a wide Texan hip brushes my upper arm, lumbers for more food.

Soon after the battery, a mild respite comes in the form of Richard, asking if he can share my table. He holds two full plates of food and a precariously balanced a cup of coffee. I say sure, distract me from this cauldron of witch cackles and candlelight cataclysmic minutia. I had just thought of that phrase and figured Richard would appreciate the poetic remark.

He grunts a laugh, sits down, starts preparing his morning meal and proceeds to eat with enthusiasm. I scan the room for any sign of Marieke, her absence oppressive. An oppressive lilt to my spine and a tactic she may be using to further rouse my interest.

Richard and I become fully enmeshed in conversation about Venus' relative strength, and just at the zenith of a compelling argument, she arrives, in full form, blonde hair long down her sides, short black skirt, black tights, hoop earrings flaring out to meet my aching eyes, green sweater draped along her arm.

She greets the guests with rapid hellos and begins to

laugh already at someone's inarticulate joke. She maintains composure, still, here on day four in Florence.

I watch her cross the room to the Texans, she says a few words, smiles again with unwilling hands clasped in front of her body. She makes her way to us, offers a vague response to Richard's question about the weather. Meanwhile, I trace the line of her thigh as she travels back to where she will choose her own breakfast. I wonder if she will eat the same thing as yesterday. I picture her eating breakfast in real life, not on this tour, figure I will fashion the image based on her food choices today.

She returns, yogurt and oranges, yes, the same. And now, a tiny Roman apartment, she in a t-shirt and loose white shorts, thick with the sweat of sleep still on her body, hair a tangled mess, uncolored lips, she sits upright in a sun-filled room, oranges and yogurt, before her day begins. I meet her outside her apartment door after breakfast, perhaps in the hallway where she won't expect me, see her delight at the surprise, and then we travel out into the day together. Such are my thoughts as Richard speaks about ancient Roman architecture.

Amid my reverie, I catch a glimpse of her stockinged legs, my eyesight meets her body directly. I can see without needing to turn my head. Her shoes twitch slightly as she struggles to peel her orange. I watch the spoon travel into and then out of her mouth.

WE LEAVE THE hotel by bus to the Galleria dell'Accademia, then walk a few blocks through dense Florentine streets to the museum. The line stretches around the corner. Marieke leaves us there to go make her arrangements.

The city street, packed with camera rolls and comfortable shoes, eyes that look skyward to catch a glimpse of architect statements, maybe a slight ray of sun as the tourists small talk in anticipation. Groups from all over the world gather here and surround my small frame. I lift my head to see above the crowd. A small, small Helen on a street corner queue knowing nothing of all these thousand people, each of them knowing nothing of her.

This feeling of alone lasts several minutes. I wait patiently for a headset and ticket. While I notice an ancient leather-bound bookstore across the street,

Marieke returns with the required gadgetry to get us safely in to see the statues. She hands out headsets, again I am sure to be last. Must appear restrained, deferential, easy to be last with no problem at all, she'll appreciate my patience, and again I will have the final word.

Her duties done, we all wait in line, chat, drink water to wet our throats still dry from early morning coffee. Marieke asks me if I am looking forward to seeing David. I say Yes, to see what all the fuss is about. I tell her, It's difficult to be excited about something so ubiquitous, but what I meant was that the Texan's enthusiasm was naturally dampening my own. I must not appear as if I have a single appreciation in common with that woman.

I tell Marieke with shy humor that the verdict is still out on David, he hasn't proven himself yet to me. She laughs, white toothed, turns her head out into the street, then looks straight back through me.

She says, You know, some people, many people, many people have fainted at just the sight of the Statue of David. I laugh, say they must have eaten some bad lasagna or something, to make light, to seem aloof, the casual gaze I project with skill and precision. I tell her I doubt I'll faint, I've seen pictures so many times, and quite frankly, I'd rather be viewing a Titian at the Uffizi right now. She smiles again, says, We'll see how you respond, you're such an artist yourself.

I realize at this moment that I have fooled her entirely with my insistence on taking photographs. Perhaps I could incorporate the deceit into some plan or another.

I simply say, Yes, we'll see.

People have fainted in front of David, I think quietly, a graven image on my own face as we inch up the line.

We linger, the line meanders up the street with a lazy attitude and bored countenance. To pass a bit of time, Richard and I visit the bookshop across the street, our hands touch thick scratched leather spines and try out the quill pens on display. A quiet world has formed here between these bookstore walls, I want to climb right in, those two volumes want me to join them. Let's see if I can make their worlds meet. I tell Richard my desire to fold myself into the book pages and he responds with a sardonic smile.

We stay as long as we can, smell of dust and age on

our skin and clothes, like how it would feel to understand Italian. My feet shuffle toward the highest stacks of books, I worry I may slip and knock them down. Anxiety is my cue to leave, so Richard and I scamper out the door to find the green sweater she wears as a beacon out to me.

WE ENTER THE building after the slow, crowded slide to the front of the line behind long blonde hair. Another guest tour guide greets us, one who will explain to us the intricacies of the sculptor's hand.

She shows us first how Michelangelo's contemporaries worked, how they used models first then carved the marble, how Renaissance artists stole materials from ancient Roman temples, the new that would become old again.

We pass by unfinished carvings that once had Michelangelo's hands all over them. He believed the figures were already within the stone, the artist's job was to free them, to burst their shapes forth fully formed from the living marble. The artist sets free what is already inside. These figures only half freed from inside, these large sinewy arms, legs cut off at the thigh, feel alive, somehow alive and breathing, willing to meet me for dinner, suffocated in their frozen limbs. They ask me to converse, to wildly surmise about tomorrow's weather, or whether the train will be on time, they reach out to me by the neck and shoulder, their half-formed arms want to pull me to the ground with immovable weight. Except I fight. I keep moving my feet. I fight against them toppling over me one by one as I make my way toward David.

RAW MATERIAL. MARBLE, our own utterance.

We enter the dome where David stands. David. I look up at his satchel and turned head, so high I am breathless, so tall I am fallen down to the ground. Unexpectedly fallen. Thighs and overlarge hands stand solid as tourists take photographs, fingers, phones, camera lenses pointed in all directions along his body.

I stand aloof with glazed eyes, there and not there, the stony legs and chest, smoothed muscle across the shoulder. The artist is in love, but that is a cliché. The size overwhelms, another cliché. Helen becomes cliché with her feet before a miracle. The tourists seem tall against my annoyance. I am David's Achilles heel attached to the limb of a tree, a slight, a perfect distribution.

David is in the shadows of a valley I cannot enter. Classical images capture an invitation, but I have no words to accept. White bone, flesh, careless in his storied body, a curled knife locked on to the veins in his throat, not carved but faded into consciousness, hands not wrenched but open, a posterior smooth with admiration. He islands absolute, superior in every way.

The problem is his face, the problem is the face. Helen's problem.

Art itself had recalled his face out from every word she had ever written, every cry of despair. The face of the artist staring down the impossible. The face of David dismantling David, the face of Helen unforgetting every word. Helen with a pencil in her hand, lying on the floor half naked, half conscious, half inside a fantasy. I stage myself inside his eye, wry terror, a holy crusade, a risen army and my name tattooed on another's chest, an angry horde beating down the door of my cell, powerful, like a single word.

Helen winces out to capture the penniless despair she is plunged into immediately and forever.

My small mouth shuns itself as I raise my own telephone to capture a small, frail picture, just to remember the moment, pitiful, the picture of my indolence, the betrayal, the grief of having never touched perfection. The grief of a life not spent in pursuit of perfection. Not creating enough, can there be enough creation to drown the impermanence, one perfect thing in one paltry life.

The worst part is that he did it. Helen's eyes now full of tears.

The artist and the face of the impossible. He did it. It's too much. It's too much for a Helen who takes pictures of young women and then steals their scarves, who touches volumes of prose she did not write. Perhaps theft is the closest thing to perfection. I am traced back to a single instant of Michelangelo.

So many flowers have not seen Helen the artist at work, years of waste and responsibility. I am broken nerves and a child. I weep openly, then turn down my head, hide my face from all the other faces, allow the heaves of my chest to happen beneath my shirt. I surrender.

IT IS TIME to make my exit, out to where Marieke waits. My feet step lightly, I turn back my head for one last look. The despair of the artist achieved in one striking image, David waiting in marble. I cannot turn my head again, there is more to think about, perhaps the only things that will ever be important in a small life. Two fewer words and all could be lost, two words may make the difference.

I cajole tears, imagining his determined eyes once more, the impossible, the possible, it's not fair. I must depart with the music of the possible, the impossible. The despair that he had done it, had made it all into that which has been done. He couldn't have proven perfection is possible because I have defended impossibility for many years. It's not possible, I would say. The threat is the possible, magic desperation of the possible, downward eyelashes of the possible, hand around the throat of the possible. Despair now an ache of desire, the way my hand moves across the air as I wipe my own tears, now infused with the possible. I will carry it all out to the gift shop and into the streets. My feet and eyes will move with the possible, my head will turn with the possible, my books will now be possible, every word will spell one thing and that is the possible. I am skin crawled with the possible, which is only the impossible given the name David.

I HAVE GIVEN over to weeping in a gift shop entryway, smiling customers buying miniature Davids and postcards to send to friends with phrases that match the clichés I myself have just uttered. I stand in a narrow entranceway next to a swivel stand of postcards, his feet, eyes, mouth, right arm, left buttock, toes slightly bent, left knee. Parts of him disenfranchised and deconstructed, each one results in an extension of tears, the crying is very much out of hand, tears that open up the coat when it is raining, tears in the nighttime woods, tears that take the train, a stranger at your side and his memory in your pocket. Strange tears, outer limits tears, uncontrolled fantasy held inside the body, bursting forth ragged and caustic, vicious and undistilled next to a spinning postcard rack and the sound of a Texan murmur.

I move more squarely into the store where images taunt me with their chants: it's perfect it's possible it's perfect it's possible it's possible it's possible it's perfect it's possible it's not possible it can't be.

Another wall, another set of scattered picture postcards, and there, just there is one of his face. The determined face of the possible pierces Helen's heart in its swollen ache, no heartbeat can respond properly enough to such beauty. I understand singularly perhaps a unique emotion. Perhaps a clichéd one. I try to make it not matter. It may be the collective energy of the place and Marieke's smile that has caused such a response, like a trick. Yet there, the knitted brow, there the lines across his forehead, perhaps only Helen has ever understood them. Arrested eyes, black jacket to face and mouth, heaves of body buried in racks of tourist detritus, I keep my eyes and face turned to the wall. My long sighs empty of savagery.

As I stand solemn and still heaving, a Texan woman strides up beside me, touching her overlarge hands to postcard images, ones that have kept me wrapped in the feeling of sublime insight, my own deep core, beauty unmistakable, I am shown myself for the first time.

The Texan is an exuberant high school teacher of English. She chatters without breath into my unwilling ear. She says, These postcards are perfect for my class, our unit on the Renaissance. You see, I teach all about David and I have the perfect idea.

She uses the word perfect.

I can use these postcards like a puzzle, you see. Here, my students will put the puzzle together to create David from the pictures of all his different parts.

Her dull eye toward me disturbs the quiet as she punctuates each gruesome word with exclamation and a twist toward the next sound. I am struck by absurdity and rage, overwhelming and new, compelled by custom to offer a small half smile, a slight nod of the head, as if to curtsy a violent attack on aesthetic sensibility.

Here is why Helen is finished. Finis, Hélène.

Helen, the inimitable voyeur, subterfuges her way through the moment, touches an illicit nerve. The aliveness becomes delicious. The Texan confirms my state of mind with a mythic postcard puzzle and a wild deficit of intellect. Each Texan fingertip swallows another of my sobs.

Dark green sweater, fingers cast into long blonde hair. I want to enter a silent hotel room, only her hands have the key.

This Texan should be wrenched down a well, every word pulled from her bloodied throat, the darkness would take each word into its maw, smother her with its obscenity. Her crime is the assault on a moment of sublime weeping, on the incipience of an imperative, the need to destroy and to create, the decision beneath the stifled sobs.

She makes her sordid purchases, returns to the street. It is my turn to find a trinket, some kitchen magnet picture postcard reminder, some profane illusion of the real. I am disgusted with myself for doing so, my ire despises me back. I have ceded control to that woman with the profane mouth in her high school classroom. She shall surely ruin tourist shops altogether.

She is not why I have come, though, now I must remember why I find myself just here, just now, with strangers and the exchange of Euros. Ancient beauty, "felt in the blood, and felt along the heart," a heart's ration of Art unburied in footsteps across cobblestone streets.

I decide after all on a postcard, exponential misery of the banal and my still sobbing features, a memento of Helen's birth, imprisoning time for a faulty memory between four flimsy corners. Yet out of these thousands, which shall I choose? Yes, it must be his face, the memory of the face must not fade, his face and solid shoulders will hang above my small desk at home, give me over to thoughts of creative genius which will only reveal themselves in artifacts of word or song, some inflection of truth scrambling onto the page. A relapse of narrative, a permanence of verse. The image replaces the real over time, David himself becomes merely the mind that recalls.

These pictures explicate the natural world, my own hands like the Texan's, grasping and flighty, undecided and awkward, unaccounted for in light that casts the wrong shadow. I am paralyzed out of joy, my weeping continues in a more orderly fashion, freshly ironed livery hung in the servant's quarters. It is nearly time to meet Marieke, I must choose before it's too late. This will do, David's face, his heart shaped eyes, eyes that will return with Helen to Marcel, to the worn gloves of motherhood, aching trips through grocery store aisles, seeing again the names of friends. This face, the striving of a mirrored image, the self in fury of birth, bloodied and bruised as it makes its new way into the world.

I pass one Euro to the cashier and receive a handful of change in return.

ONCE OUTSIDE, THE street accepts me into its epiphany.

Richard and Marieke wait for me, speaking to each other in tones of joy to the side of the building. I emerge weak, unresolved, and make my way to them. Richard sees my dark black coat, reddened eyes and cheeks, I try to hide them but it's too late, they betray me, full of gloom, a lost moment, still the tears will not stop, my veined neck reveals my state of mind.

The surface textures of stone facades and faded bookstore windows haunt me with the mantra of the possible. Richard asks me if I'm okay. I say, Yes, just overwhelmed, and as I say the word I again must bury my worn face in my hands. I veil my weeping on the way to the Duomo.

Richard, in a gesture of comfort says There There, makes sure I don't lose my way as the tour group winds its way through old, crowded streets. His kindness contributes to my unearthing while I follow his footsteps with precision. I cannot look up for myself. His feet escort my elaborate revelation toward the Gates of Paradise. I forget the skin on my teeth, the pencil in my hand will remove all traces of before. These untested hypotheses may disappear tomorrow when we arrive in Assisi, yet right now, I seem to be etched into these bronze doors, ones only gods can enter.

My head is turned away from the Gates, from hands of ancient Roma, from the green and pink of cathedral walls. The massive Gates appreciate their own grand physique, but I am chained inside four walls with Michelangelo, his smooth looks and insolence about the shape of David's nose. The cathedral tiles across the way share their heavy weight with me. We are both a thousand times sunk, our feet disappear.

The Duomo, the artist now Brunoshetti, his dome an architectural impossibility, he too shares the weight of the possible. These old spires, they point away from me, their unfailing is the bend to David's right hand, pierced reflection, stony eyes and legs.

The sobbing loss, waned, fallen into tears that escape in their own time. I have missed communion with the Gates, with the Duomo. I tell myself I must come back someday, must bring Marcel, he must see this for himself to be destroyed along with me. I send him a message that simply states Cried at David. He is asleep and won't receive it until later, when I am eating dinner with Marieke.

We take a break outside the Duomo for pictures. I take none. I stand unimpressed at the thought of an image, David's eyes pierce the illusion of them, illuminate the necessity of the three-dimensional.

At the side of the church, the blackened concrete meets the pink of the dusty lower tiles. Another body steps near, it is Marieke, beside me to look at the Dome, to ask if I have recovered from seeing David, laughing in small sounds as her arm reaches toward my shoulder in comfort. She says, I told you people sometimes fainted. I can only manage a saddened sound, It's just, perfect, perfect, it shouldn't be possible, can't be. She laughs again with the taste of empathy, squeeze to my shoulder in material affection. Her playful mockery, And you thought you wouldn't be affected. I look at her eyes and tell her You were right all along. I say her name once and return my eyes to the Duomo.

WE WIND OUR way through ramshackle Florentine streets and storefronts, arrive at the Piazza Santa Croce. Marieke tells us that inside the church are Michelangelo's remains, he's buried there within its walls. She tells me alone this story, which I know because of the way her earrings catch the light. We won't go in, she says, unless the group wants to, but it's expensive, and she thought instead we could use the time to do some shopping. She points us in the direction of a leather shop across the square, tells us it's some of the finest leather in Italy.

No doubt, she gets a cut. I admire her cunning and

meticulous redirection, Machiavellian exchange over dead animal skins. Her ethic amuses me as I enter the shop, vaguely bored, averting my eyes from the red leather jacket in the corner. The thick leather scent destroys the memory of David's white body, so I leave the shop, take a seat on a bench outside.

A few minutes later, Marieke joins me, she and I alone. I have nothing particularly interesting to say, the silence of the piazza having overtaken me, so I ask her questions about her life, her youth, college years, high school. I want to know every time her teeth have showed. She tells me the story of a high school project about the Amish population of America, recounts an embarrassing skit she and a classmate performed as part of the project. She lets me into her shyness, her regrets over words she has said in the context of a school project.

Rejoice with me as we sit outside the Santa Croce, where St. Francis made his mark in a swamp outside the walls of the city. Here, where his feet first said Yes, this soil is what we must take for ourselves, here is the ground we must claim. Helen fuses the two, her aching feet and the feet of St. Francis, bare and bony and full of snags. The ache of sandaltops as they cross over the skin, here as my silent half smile gives way to dark fantasy. St. Francis beckons me over with him, into the marsh land, to take a vow of poverty.

This beautiful irony would likely be lost on Marieke, so I say nothing of it. Instead, I ask her more questions, her family, her hometown, the walls of her adolescent bedroom, any romantic attachments in Rome. I leave this question for last. She tells me No, just as Richard exits the shop to join us. St. Francis with a bag of leather goods in place of a rosary.

We all decide to eat lunch at a restaurant across the square.

THE RESTAURANT CATERS to tourists, outdoor heaters ready for us to enjoy. A respite from the cold, a warm nose instead of a cold one, we sit and each cheese pizza along with others from our tour group.

Marieke's attention wanders, but she is full of duty. Each voice at the table calls for her attention, her bored, tired attention. I stay quiet, focus instead on the heat radiating toward my skilled body, on the cup of hot tea I have ordered which I cradle in my hands with a cherished breath to cool it. I look around for a voice that doesn't bore me but every sound is too full of leather and gelato.

After the meal, I escape the small sounds of laughter and slink around the plaza alone, insulation to remedy loneliness. Before I leave the restaurant, I ask when and where we are to meet. She tells me, Let's meet at the bench, in thirty minutes? She asks me a question – thirty minutes? – a question, she seeks my approval. I offer it to her, say Yes, that shall do, and have set her afternoon in stone with a single syllable.

The piazza, stunned quiet, seems to have absolved the energy of voice. The silence hollow, I attempt to find a shop worth peering into for a moment. No bookshops here, no unlined notebooks, only high-end merchandise shipped in from elsewhere, busy tourists dressed inappropriately for the weather.

I decide to venture out, just a little, not too far. A side street, determined and crooked, finds itself in front of me, offering up a woman who sells from a cart various sizes and shades of fabrics, ones that might be fashioned into skirts, shawls, scarves, headdresses. She smiles, I return her look, grateful for her presence.

My fingertips embrace the softness of the fabric, consider for a moment a purchase. And then, an idea, one infused with generosity, and genius. A perfect plan, I have come upon my own perfection.

I have only a few minutes, so I choose rather spontaneously a large grey and white scarf with gleams of light blue, pink, just for an edge of color. It is an easy choice, really. The scarf is not for me, not for my own cold neck, nor for surreptitious images stolen of me.

The woman is paid with several coins, after which I consider the logical implications of returning with only one scarf. Perhaps I should, after all, purchase this moment for myself, too, if for no other reason than to appear nonchalant, buying scarves all over town, in fact, just for the sake of brilliance dazzling in bright blue and yellow fabric, commemoration in a dark blue shawl.

Yet to do so, I remain convinced, would destroy the moment, which is simply too delicious to take for myself. The woman's cart on a small, crooked street, a gift of cloth tipped in Marieke's direction.

The meeting time arrives. I take myself and the small paper bag over to the bench where we two shared our histories. She is there alone, only a few others scattered beyond her. The perfection of the moment is too easy, it is the figures themselves buried in stone aching to be freed, the delight of a warm smile when you make it here after midnight.

I quickly say her name, say I was just over there, around that corner and there was a lively stand with a very kind old woman selling fabrics. I say, I heard you asking the hotel manager about a scarf, I noticed you weren't wearing one and it is very cold. I say, I got this for you as a thank you for showing me David. It was such a perfect day, I say.

Her mouth opens in surprised appreciation. I see her tongue when she says Oh, that's very sweet, such a beautiful color, how kind of you, so lovely and so similar to the one I had lost.

My own tongue responds too simplistically for the moment. I'm glad you like it. And then, I hope your neck is as appreciative as you are. We laugh at the apathy of this sad personification.

She wraps the whole scarf like magic around her thin white neck, spreads her long hair across the fabric, bundles and wraps its length in long curled layers that I cannot mimic. She is too clever, she cannot be matched.

Marieke, curled around the scarf I have touched, the one she will wear now for the rest of the trip. Helen the mythic has rescued her cold neck in return for her consolations, her pointed toe suspended in David's direction. You see, Helen is a clever one, too, Marieke. She, too, knows how to curve a pretty scarf gently around a neck.

I FOLLOW HER cozy new look all the way to the Uffizi, each step full of purpose. The coming night under my feet echoes into my arms and thighs, into my own neck now sullen with only a weightless semi-soft fabric to keep it warm, so far from her luxury. The streets have gone grey with clouds, my hands swing at my sides, a metronome accompaniment to the glances of passersby. I count methodically the number of successes that may still be in store for me today.

The museum, the Uffizi, it wallows in a stupor of Art, indulgences seen only in picture postcards or grand heavy books on the Italian Renaissance. I wander into its wallowing, a priceless caravan of untethered bodies passes by, swearing their allegiance to me. I hear the storm outside and inside, all the bare-breasted Venuses call out my name, Helen, Helen, I hear on their lips and in the lines of their stomachs, thick round flesh, vacant erotic eyes, deft hands painted in place of a pubis. My feminist side wants to balk but I am too much in love with every line, I have no time for protestations.

In searching for Titian's Venus of Urbino, I think about the unknown intellectual side of Venus of Botticelli, imagine her reading Shakespeare after dark, Milton on a warm afternoon.

I wander the museum with a searching gesture, and in the distance see Marieke, scarf to her side, sitting on a bench in the grand hallway. My guide through the Renaissance in a long green sweater sits cross-legged to show me the length of her black stockings.

The question comes out full English teatime bravado, My good lady, Do you happen to know in which room Titian's Venus lives?

Yes, laugh again for me, Marieke, tell me how you like the way I talk.

She laughs for me, tells me she likes the way I talk. I respond with a coy, Why I'm so happy it pleases you, Mademoiselle, pretend tip of the hat and shuffle of feet.

As her head and hand point me in the right direction, I do not ask her why she is sitting instead of looking. It would be an amateur's question. Of course she's not looking, she studied art history for one year in Florence, she has walked these halls many times, has seen it all already, seen them all, a regular Prufrock on a stockinged bench. In the room the women come and go, talking of Michelangelo, the mermaids singing each to each, they sing to Marieke now, I can tell by the color in her cheeks as she turns her head away from me.

For thirty minutes, Venus of Urbino admires the length of my hair, while I admire the gentle way she both buries and exhumes her own pleasure. A gesture of modesty and masturbation, one party indulges the other, the hand that covers also the hand that touches, the hand that steals the hand that gifts, always the perpetration of a more illicit game. Titian's brush strokes teach me a methodology of obsession, a syntax of persuasion, an introductory course in how quiet backgrounds go unobserved.

I wait for too long there with Venus, grifting her secrets, suddenly our time at the Uffizi is over. I am told to meet the group outside, I must leave Titian here.

Outside, Richard has found his wonderfully cocksure, two-footed stance. I join him there, strike my feet to the ground, too, ask him how he enjoyed the museum. He says he quite liked seeing the Birth of Venus again after so many years but found the Caravaggio's quite disturbing. In response, I admit that all the bared breasts held my attention and as a result was only able to glance through the gruesome Caravaggio room. Perhaps I will find some Caravaggio ornament that can return home with me, a little memento of what was lost.

We plan to wander the nearby streets of Florence for a couple of hours before meeting again at the hotel to get ready for dinner. Hours, such a long word, time with an intimation of delay.

Richard and I decide to team up, explore a street market full of cheaply manufactured goods that each still feel somehow unique, in that tourist sort of way, when you are aware that everything on display has no intrinsic value but will, at some point, become the purveyor of quite a pleasant memory.

Along the tendrilled lines of watchbands purse strings necklaces leather goods candlesticks figurines candies, I wonder if Marcel has gotten my text message from earlier. I think about the fun we'd be having if he were here, how we'd likely both vie for Marieke's attention, make a game out of who can win her over, touch her arm first, tally how many times each of us make her laugh, friendly, but serious competition. He'd win, and I'd be jealous. A complicated jealousy, her attentions toward him, her diminished attentions toward me, his eyes turned elsewhere, his intolerable ability to dash out lines from nowhere that showcase his wit. It's best he's not here, better she be all my own. Besides, I'll need stories to tell him, stories to render me a mystery. Helen the mystery. Mystery. Mister-E. Miss-Tree. The word manipulates me into purchasing at random a small red leather bracelet from a tangled kiosk nearby. Deep red leather, thin white wrist, emblems of the unexpected.

MARIEKE IS GLAD to have her scarf as we walk as a large group to dinner. The rain has no remorse, like the book page of a fairy tale, the lonely princess stands ragged, cold on the steps of the local blacksmith. The old rain follows our footsteps all the way across alleyways, along tiny side streets, looks both ways just in time, offers no respite when we're told to wait outside for fifteen minutes. My raincoat with its sturdy black hood mocks sympathy for the high school girls who arrive with no jackets whatsoever.

We are finally seated at a long table, the candlelit center of a side room in the restaurant. Marieke has nowhere to sit but by my side. I smile in earnest, and say, We've saved a place for you here. Water pours onto the street outside, beats the worn red awning that hangs just outside. The waiter opens the full-length window and insists that we've made the safest escape.

Marieke sends out a question to the table. What were your favorite artworks today? The question mark hangs suspended until my voice meets it at the corner store.

Most certainly David, I say, in hopes of sounding my unique flair but realizing my utter failure. I strike for a new note, tell her I quite liked roaming around the Uffizi as well, gaping at the Titians. At last, the right chord.

We begin discussing commerce and art, whether the two had ever made a good pair, for the topic is tragedy on an epic scale. Her wine glass listens intently to the conversation, I can tell by the lazy glint on its surface that it is unimpressed. I change the subject slightly, Is a painting an object, or a force of energy? Perhaps, I say, true artistic purity only exists in paintings burned in attic fires, in the living pulse that remains without the corruptive force of the material world. She affirms the sentiment with a nod while white wine touches her lips. The one strand of hair that clings to her face agrees, too, as if folded into a lined notebook page full of grand ideas. Her fingers disapprove of the argument full stop, so I spend the next few minutes silently making amends.

My conversational acumen entices her into my affections, offers relief from these English-teaching gnat-toothed vultures vying for her attention. We talk between bits of cheese, watch whole legs of cooked chicken put before other faces, eye our disgust at the torn flesh in their mouths, carcasses down the gullets of feeble brains without a single understanding of the alphabet.

Meanwhile, I try to convince Marieke that any consideration of audience corrupts the truth of the artist's vision. She counters with the argument that obstructions, such as audience and genre, often become catalysts for artistic invention. I cannot disagree, and thereafter am mildly offended by her display of sound intellect, sharp like the lightning outside.

My indolent fingers grasp a wine glass, ready to counterpoint, when from nowhere the lights go out in the restaurant. Thumbnail candle flames offer just enough light to engage in collective laughter as we realize the power has gone out. The fates are treating us to a proper medieval Italian evening dinner party. We should likely thank them for their kindness.

Marieke rises to check with the restaurant manager, she must take care of the business while we all carry the merriment toward our good fortune. Richard laughs with the Texan teacher and her Texan friend. The young girls text message home and to friends, while the large man on our tour converses with a woman at the table across from us.

Our table is fruitfully engaged in lights out dinner joy, the sound returned after brilliant silence.

Marieke's empty seat, plate of pasta in sauce sitting half eaten at the table, half full glass of wine and napkin placed silently alongside her plate.

It is dark except for the faint glow that renders us silhouette. Marieke is across the room speaking in serious tones with the head waiter. My eye catches her fork, which has been in her mouth, now resting there as a taunt, a mocking tone. A genius move has been revealed. Genius, Helen!

I look around to confirm my anonymity. Then, out goes my hand, slowly, almost involuntary, a decided action from long ago mythic realms, an inevitability, reaction instead of action. I put two fingertips around the unsuspecting utensil, quickly exchange it with my own, both buried in pasta now just as before, each hiding its secrets in the belly of a wide-rimmed bowl.

The switch has been made, flawless, a work of art, she couldn't possibly know, my technique has been carved from stone since Da Vinci. The exchange made, I wrap several small strands of my own meal around the fork, bring it slowly to my mouth. I have only one chance to feel her tongue before my own corrupts its purity, I must savor the seconds it takes until the fork is in my mouth fully and without a tinge of modesty. I slowly indulge, remove the fork slowly from around my lips, chew slowly, look over to see her faint shadow in the dark. The table talks along as if nothing happened, blindly masticating animal flesh and predicting when the lights will return.

After a few minutes she returns, sits down and tells us all the lights should be on again in a few minutes, the lightning storm, the generator, the restaurant manager says this and that. I can hardly focus on the situation at hand because I am more interested in when she will pick up her fork, buried in her plate of food, which has now gone cold. I hope the chill doesn't dissuade her from taking at least one more bite.

Her speech finished, she takes a drink of water. The glass glistens in admiration of me. She takes up her fork, turns long strands of pasta around the tongs with her spoon, then places a full, elaborate mouthful solid and beautiful and elegant into her mouth. She chews, cheeks full of satisfaction.

WE LEAVE THE restaurant, the rain, impossible to ignore, outplays me at my forceful game. Marieke leads us to a bus stop a few blocks away, waiting in step to the raindrops beating down on our unprepared bodies. An impromptu bus in the Florentine dark thrills us all into excited chatter. Richard shouts a grand Hooray! as he empties the brim of his hat of water. I stick by his side for the comfort of laughter and a side quip or two, the feeling of alone abated for a few minutes along the bus path. He flirts shyly with Italian women on the bus, tells them all this weather is too much for an Englishman, Jolly Goods his way into their affectionate smiles. So many ways to gain other eyes.

The bus, full of wild energy, delights in our wet bodies, ourselves full of food and wine. We all lunge into stops and starts as the bus navigates narrow crowded city streets.

Back at the hotel, a dampened display of garments tells Marieke how much of an adventure she brought us on with her. We quickly find our rooms for the night, disrobe, find some warm way to remove our scarves and wet shoes.

My hotel room steams with condensation as I remove my wet clothing, dry my short hair with a towel, run the towel over my chest and legs to warm the skin. The air is warm, a warm glow fills the room from the hum of the bathroom light.

I make sure the washcloth is still in place, check to see if any other tiles have mysteriously fallen. In this room, bored Helen does not want to read a book and has had Marieke in her mouth.

To pass the time, I dig to the bottom of my suitcase, unwrap her scarf from its plastic, and lay it out flat on the bed. I lay on the quiet bed, too, embrace the darkness, pull the fabric to my face and neck, across the length of my body, into my touch, breasts to its soft shape, legs closed around its folds. I am wrapped in the breath of Marieke, unfolding then folding her around my arms and legs. Outside, I hear a siren, and a low hum of voice, silence remains waiting in the hallway outside my door. The sound of my breath next to hers pierces the unlit air.

I put my finger in my mouth, imagine it is hers. I place my wet fingers on my chest, then slowly down the flesh of my still-dampened body. She is trapped between my legs and now wrapped around my throat. I slowly indulge in the softened sounds against my skin, feel the wetness of her lips along my breast and inner thigh, place my fingers around and inside her, pulse us both to a long slow burning climax of wet hands wet teeth wet neck warm with embrace. My hands feel the strength of her as I clutch the stolen clothing, find its resting place between my legs. I drift into a long, tired sleep, waking only once at two am to set my alarm for the morning.

Day Five
Assisi

THE MORNING CAME quick, its arms full of desire to stay warm in bed. I resign, unwrap my body from the night. The floor's cold attitude compels me to give up my plans for the day, whatever they might have been. Perhaps all these games have no place in Assisi. Nerves in my feet press down to an ache as I look at the small red clock at the bedside. Twenty minutes to shower and prepare, pack the suitcase neatly, close all the drawers, verify again there is no one behind the missing tile. I must remember to remove the washcloth and feign nonchalance.

My phone carries messages to me from Marcel, from our tiny home, from the footfalls I can almost hear on our worn carpet he tries so diligently to keep clean.

He asks, How are things, How is Florence, How are

you, How was David, and he attaches pictures of the children for my amusement and for his own. They are wearing the cowboy costumes we bought them for Christmas, dressed for a scene they're all filming, making a film all together, a collaboration without the Mom, who is instead sabotaging long blonde hair in Italy.

Marcel and the boys, the energy of creation infuses our dust worn house, our tiny rooms that smell faintly of cat urine but nobody minds, piles of books and art supplies reveal our love of each other, remind us all that we are artists after all, nothing can assail our bodies or minds.

In the photograph, the two boys look with intensity at a camera they've placed precisely to capture their old-time main street duel, pictures they drew for the set hang crooked on the wall.

Marcel guides them into our world of subterfuge, we call our lives stories, the detached presence of the observing eye trains itself on an unsuspecting world. We tell them there is nothing more important than to create, that the life of the artist is cruel and self-perpetrating, isolated and of necessity ignored by the unconcerned masses. We tell them we create for ourselves, for no one else, for the purity of a single artistic impulse, which, trained in the proper aesthetic, and with a genetic disposition toward excellent taste, will give them joy and contentment unimaginable. The life in these pictures is the one I have left and the one to which I will always return.

I respond to Marcel in letters much less adequate than the pictures require, if I were writing a story my response would seem trenchant, obtuse even, or at the very least unimpressed. I cannot get my mind to find a guise or gesture of appreciation, the mind too hazy glazed over with the morning cup of coffee I have not yet embraced. I tell him simply, The pictures are adorable. I miss you all, so much. A trifle compared to the infusion of home and art the images offer me as we set out for Assisi.

MARIEKE SITS ALONE for breakfast along the far side of the room, peels her orange slowly, takes one bite at a time. Is she purposefully sitting as far away from me as possible? Is the morning her moment of repose from the roving eyes that want to drown her, to pull her into my equations, to see how precisely her flesh enters creation by my hands?

My encounter with David must have set her off in another direction, sat her down across the room without a good morning, without attending to the intelligent conversation I have brought her this week. She becomes the scent of peeled oranges and yogurt, blue jeans and a white shirt that when she stands upright shows the slightest taste of belly skin.

I look at the pictures Marcel sent while I eat my pastry as a form of aggression against her, to tell her she has fallen from my favor with the absence of Hello. Yes, today will be different. The story of today will be one slight for another. She will see how the town feels without my attentions, she will have only bulging Texan bodies and the vacant apathies of college girls on their telephones. Yes, today is not for her, but for Assisi, for Helen's patron saint who induces a desire for the medieval, for brightly illuminated manuscripts impossible to read but beautiful.

I eat my breakfast in silence, take my leave without looking even a glance in her direction.

On the bus again, the narrow seat cushions nurture me to sleep, assist me in organizing yesterday's events. The smooth grey interior draws me in close to the middle of the bus. I triumph today in choosing a seat without regard for Marieke's location. Today, I am for Italy. I am not for a trace of fingertip held over a seat back, or an ephemeral voice announcing banalities over a crackling microphone.

She stands to talk even while the bus is moving, sways back and forth and to the side with the inertia underneath.

The more aggressive members of our tour bus make the attempt to talk regardless of the fact that it's the morning. Voices swirl around the early air, dusting off shelves, moving around the curtains. Helen is the room with a Polanski film, grim with the noise of human bodies, irritated with fumbling hands that cannot rightly grasp a book.

I try to drown it all out by searching through my backpack for nothing in particular. At the bottom, two crushed granola bars, brought from home, a reasonable gesture but now a crumbled mass at the bottom of a bag, a memory of a moment of caution. I find the heads of two Lego men, more than a few pebbles of cat litter, nothing of too much interest.

I settle on the Highsmith novel that has been neglected now for two days, pages marred by constant motion, yellowed with age on our shelf. Highsmith, catalyst for romantic adventure, pennies thrown down in despair could not rouse her from the attentive eyes she casts as Helen plots out her next move.

Except, no plotting today, I must remind myself to remove the stimuli, then to look for any change.

I read a few lines from a middle chapter that seem to be set in the town where we last stopped, but the words cause deep fatigue. Raincoat again a pillow, I curl up small and drift to sleep, engine hum and mottled voices waylaid by an unseen ancillary anger. We will soon be near Assisi, Helen's origin story, her uniform and formerly shaved head.

I expect the vista over which the town looks to be a grand escapade, but instead it's a cold hand on the back of my neck, a slight buckle in the small of my back, a set of eyes craned too far to the left to hit the target. We arrive in Assisi by way of a winding hill up to the city, regard the landscape with checkered disappointment. Assisi seems swollen on a hillside, magical, majestic, yet destitute as a tour bus parking lot. The vista, a lovely photo, but alone, small, distant, untouched by Assisi's rent garments.

We will remain in this town for several hours, have a bit of lunch, tour St. Clare's chapel and the basilica. A sunny day in Assisi warrants a set of mild predicaments. Sweater or jacket? Small purse or large? The sadly worn raincoat seems inappropriate for the occasion, as if the presence of Marieke has downgraded the beloved to become the despised. Assisi would appreciate the gesture, but next to Marieke and the freshly applied lipstick of the Texans, holes in pockets give Helen the air of the slovenly, the oversized, the gluttonous who hides it all under cover of night. Short red hair grown four weeks long causes deep enough seclusion, but the black coat underwhelms my desire to be regarded with a tinge of pleasure.

I begin the answer with the question.

How cold is it outside?

How will I desire to feel while participating in the mocking of Assisi with a pocketful of change and the apathy of hidden desire?

A split-second decision must be made as we all alight from the bus, a sweater in one hand, jacket in the other. Perhaps both just in case? Yet perhaps the chill will necessitate joyful renunciation, discomfort to approximate the negation of St. Francis, indulgence in a day of misery absent of comforts that give false witness. Yes, perhaps the raincoat should remain. St. Francis would approve.

However, I would be cold.

A slight breeze enters the bus, the air bites the side of my cheek, the decision is made. The universe reassures me yet again in a sign unasked for and crawling up the stairs of a bus. Jacket and sweater and large bag to carry a book just in case a moment of quiet needs to be filled. A choice born of utilitarian philosophy can never be trusted. A dimmed decision, beleaguered by open windows, a sign of peace, a signal to the gods that I am still listening, a plea to keep making themselves known to me. I am an obedient servant to their whims.

THE WALK INTO the town is a solemn, quiet affair. The sun hangs low even at midday, the view below disappears behind pristine monuments to a town that once kept a saint in a brick cell.

We march through the town like Marieke's well-worn charges, wait for her instructions, cede it all to her, each step, each bit of food and each drink of wine, each artwork at her commission, each of us under her tutelage. I am in love with the irony of my own domination.

I sit again on a ledge in an idle moment. Shadows cast themselves into geometry just outside St. Francis's cell, his body against the brick wall as he devoted himself to majestic poverty, a sublime commitment to himself in love. I witness winding steps down to his childhood home, feel the damp darkness, step into his piety, his chastity, his affection for St. Clare.

Finally, I must leave this space, so I walk outside and sit on a ledge to wait for the others. Stillness. I am braced for more questions. St. Francis as Art, the frescoes, the rope around his waist, absolute godlike disavowal of the material despite bare feet in the cold rain.

Would it be possible to live an ascetic life, the life of the mystic, but instead of god, I worship Art? I imagine myself translating hymns and verses from religious texts into teachings about how to celebrate the holy spirit of Art. In Art we trust...Hallowed be thy name...thy will be done...Art is the glory and the power. Art, the great redeemer, sanctified, the Savior. I'm in love with myself as a mystic, revel in the romance of a candle-lit cell. Each pen stroke, each flick of the brush, another prayer, love for creation channeled into Being, the world brings its miracles to life, reveals its perfections through devotion, the practice of symmetry, abstraction. Samuel Beckett must have understood profoundly the will of his namesake, murdered in a cathedral, memorialized in a poet's play. The incipience of a belief in my throat, I anticipate an utterance to Marcel, he will paint the flecks of color in my eyes with enthusiasm and a sense of adventure.

I am arrested by the desire to capture an image just now, to marry aesthetic understanding with a revelation.

Marieke, walking toward me, head tilted downward, reading and moving, one single ray of sunlight shines her path through the mottled buildings in castaway patterns, one single ray of light captures her body and its outstretched arms, blond hair blazing out across the lane, a cheek filled with the sun's desire, darkness now ignorant of what the sun illuminates. Alone, still, singular, I reach for my camera to cast the image into stone.

David himself could not contextualize her idle moment, which has become my epiphany. Her body now an icon, a graven image, a painted landscape with darkness behind her in a paradox by Titian, denuded and alive, solid as the granite in my penciltip that takes shape into words, rendered neutral and cast only in the light I offer her. Her feet, splendid in their eternal movement toward me, revel in my vast intelligence. Her meaning, my artistic impulse. She hardly exists outside it. She stands alone, devoted to the eye that regards her, paints her into its portrait, sees the flawless moment when her hair touches her forehead. Yes, this is the image for the ages, this will do finely, halted in this sublime moment of tension. She will never be as meaningful as she is before the eyes of Helen, the artist goddess, who creates the story others will tell of her. She is transported now into the heavens with me, her creator, standing on seashells, and lying naked in a bed.

WE PLAN TO eat lunch before visiting Assisi's tomb, the monastery, Giotto, the crypt. I join Richard and few others in a tiny two-story café. The town center, perfect in its love of windowsill flowers and silent storefronts, where the word quaint meets the mystery of the medieval in bricks that line tiny alleyways. I am haunted here by the mind and spirit. I search for logic between the walls of the ancient village.

The second floor of the restaurant is cramped and loud, thick with tour group festivities, wine guzzled down by the glass, leaps and grunts to mimic gaiety. Our entire group fits around two small tables. Richard and I allow two of the younger girls to join us, along with a few members of the tour to whom we haven't yet spoken. The room is guessed lyrics of Italian radio songs, menus read phonetically, memories of 1980s movies and television sitcom theme songs. Helen, italicized by the unknown, engages in conversation, unearthed as fossils unburied from clay.

The waitress is pretty, so I try to catch her eye. Richard impresses her more thoroughly, though, with his boisterous English flair and his willingness to take too long to order. He teases the young girls for not knowing Latin, and they laugh. My equal attempts at humor are met with sore, ambivalent eyes.

Meanwhile, even here in this small restaurant, my need to urinate outweighs my paranoia over the logistics of such a necessity. I have no choice. We will soon be in Francis's sanctuary, the last place Helen would dare use the restroom. It must be here, and now.

I climb up the narrow winding staircase to the top floor where the waitress has directed me. The dark wall, lined with portraits, reminds me of young Stephen Dedalus's walk to meet the headmaster, all those faces of authority daring him to make a sound.

At the top of the stairs, a landing, and two doors, one closed slightly, and one closed tight.

I should choose the closed door, wait for it to open.

Yet the other door, only loosely held in place, may be a reasonable indicator of vacancy. Impossible decision.

Not wanting to be caught waiting before a perfectly empty restroom doorway, I take two steps over, knock lightly at the tenuous door, brush my hand against the door handle, and realize the situation has left my control. The door opens wider, nothing to be done to stop it, so quickly, wider still, an unexpected inevitability. A young man's voice, low clear to the throat, trousers down, feet firm to the floor above the urinal.

Why, why had I opened the door?

I had no good answer.

I thought about Marieke, then about convincing the waitress to leave the restaurant with me.

He looks over his shoulder, humiliation preens itself on my cheeks.

I turn, walk quickly downstairs, tell the group I think I'll wander through the street shops for a while. I take one hurried bite of food as I depart, still in need of a toilet. My bag and jacket coward into the air with me. The man must still be in the bathroom, so I make sure to move fast, avoid another encounter.

Still hungry, still aching bladder, I sneak through streets and wonder what will be for dinner.

The streets stutter alongside me, make their way in and out of trinkets that pass for shops, nothing but tourist drivel to sully their pristine corners.

The café on the corner seems unoccupied, perfect but strange, one side of the room brimming with smells of espresso and bright gelato colors, the other side desolate and empty of product, forlorn, dreaming of its twin sister, wrapped in flakes of cigarette ash and grime.

A young barista gives me the key to the bathroom. Because of its location on the deserted side of the cafe, I am alarmed that the lock closes with such ease. How can one trust such a lock, so willing to please, but abandoned? I prop my foot against the door, worried my awkward position will end up in soiled clothing. Now, it is done. The bathroom exit, the finale, brings a release from trauma, anxiety, inhibition, the ache beneath my shoulder blades.

Coffee and pastry again, again alone at a table unable to speak Italian. The radio station plays Cyndi Lauper overhead, wistful meditation of home, memories of a 1980s childhood that sticks like tendrils.

Time to meet Marieke, I swallow the last sip of coffee, mumble a quick Grazie, hope I made myself understood.

WE ENCIRCLE HER as I am made aware of my obsession, tempered by the trepidation in my hands. Mine is an obsession of sight. Marieke narrates the life of Assisi, his stint as a military soldier, recusing his father's money, the mythology of the potato sack. I love these stories but cannot hear the words past her fingers. They are long, pink, ungloved, bristling almost red in the cold. She has pulled her sleeves down just past her wrists, but her fingers remain bare, exposed to me. She clenches them for effect, holds them open in dramatic flair, they do the talking, amused with their own pinkishness, stubborn in refusing the climb up her warm sleeve, they mesmerize the crowd, and look out toward another Assisi.

Her hands stop moving. The story is over.

The sun has found me again in the plaza in front of the basilica of St. Francis. We wait for our tour guide, who will be a resident Franciscan monk, but for now we remain captive to the armed guards who patrol at their stations and check our bags as we enter. I did not expect guns and ammunition in Assisi, but I suppose one can never be too careful.

The desperate cold reminds me that one never can tell the character of the person sitting beside you. We all should have kept that in mind while eating our snacks at lunchtime, the arched walkway perfect in its symmetry, arches a model of isolated uniformity cast, a capital letter and end punctuation all in one.

Shadows cast their angles all over the court as if a page from a geometry textbook, this one obtuse and that one the threat of isosceles. The quiet in the square seems to discuss the rise of gothic architecture. I consider capturing an image of it all, but I have already stolen a perfection in a beam of light so the rest would be pure gluttony.

The monk arrives, begins by helping us all procure our headsets. We are surprised to learn that the man is a native of Pittsburgh, not at all the vision of Franciscan piety and sacrifice the stories reveal. How have you done it, the group asks, though I never would, how have you renounced it all? Such a juvenile question. He repeats, How have I? It was really quite easy, he says, for you become used to life without the comforts of Western living. He tells us he used to be a traveling salesman. I join in the wonder, how is such a complete reversal possible? Is a life truly as grand as all that?

Helen is officially fascinated, fear and joy in the possibility that she could access the same passion if she were to renounce it all and pursue a life in Art.

He speaks in measured tones in his brown robe, explains that one of the joys of service here is that he gets to stare at the frescoes for hours as he tries to solve their mysteries. A spiritual life conducted in faded paint on walls of the basilica. My own mysteries may be solved here, too, I think. I take my seat near the back of the central nave, attempt to make as little sound as possible.

This monk tells us the same stories that Marieke's cold hands had just recounted, and I wonder if they are true or simply passed down through the ages by uninspired tour guides. Our myths transmitted by way of some worn copy machine in a travel agency back office.

The basilica will make itself known through its art, we are told.

I see young girls' teeth grow white in mockery and boredom. I want to staple their eyelids shut.

In the first-floor central chamber, the monk is storyteller muse, narrating tales hidden in his favorite paintings, all symbolic and finely constructed to reveal to the illiterate the story of the church's namesake. They still work on us, these images, their treachery held solid in each anecdotal moment of St. Francis's life. The fresco just behind the monk holds my fascination, although the monk is off to describe a different panel. How could he not discuss this picture, in which a woman is either falling or being thrown from a second story window while no one looks on, she falls alone and head first among a crowd of the disaffected? I cannot fathom the meaning and I wish the monk would explain.

Has she committed a sin of some kind? Or had she been celebrating St. Francis's arrival when she mistakenly propels herself out the open window? Did she find herself in a bedroom with an unrighteous suitor? Or is she pregnant with his child? Is she simply a woman on a mission toward suicide, absent of a priest who can absolve her?

I face the leaping woman as all other heads turn away. He is making a mistake, this monk, he keeps making a mistake by refusing her. Somehow, the secret is inside this woman who is most certainly about to die.

I start to form a question about the painting, but before I can speak he is off to another room.

We walk into the upper chamber to see Giotto's panels, only the monk tells us they aren't exactly Giotto, that he may have only designed them. I wonder who these others were who took the orders and carried them to perfection. What is an artist who designs and then says you there, you do it all while I sit here and measure out yardsticks?

A slight deflection from these thoughts comes in the form of a memory. An afternoon spent in the college library with a book of Giotto's paintings, his demon bodies contorted into a daytime reverie. Suddenly, I wish I was still there on that cloudy day. Here I am reminded only of the fraudulent nature of artistic impulse. We are frauds, we artists, telling lies and calling on others to wash our feet.

St. Francis's crypt and worn clothing is next on the tour.

Helen wishes to be St. Francis in a potato sack, walking the plank over a stony sea. Her functional yet somewhat dowdy uniform is an approximation of his, which he must have worn even in the cold like today. The patchwork canvas now hangs there on a wall, thin and absurd without a body, I myself am the pins that hold the fabric tight to the wall, there I am, pinned and wriggling, an unexpected tedium at the cliché she has become.

Marieke lurks in the periphery, waits for deliverance, her bored shoulders want to be looking at her watch.

St. Francis of Assisi's threadbare tunic hangs suspended, wonders if I am real. I wonder the same. Could this truly be the habit of St. Francis, how could they possibly know such a thing? I am immediately suspicious, but then reconsider my line of thinking. What does it matter whether it is truly real or some burgeoning capitalist's abomination? Only the romance matters now, the symbol, the truth not in the material but in the mind of the observer.

The place goes quiet, plunged into empty solitude, voiceless mist, even the Texans have only whispered secrets as they head outside to contrive the day.

Melancholy turns to disquiet as I wait patiently for a sublime renaissance, the benign smock must speak to me, the saint himself will meet me here any moment to give me a way forward.

Perhaps my belief in reincarnation is the cause for the silence. Or perhaps a general disdain for Christianity, except for a few Christians throughout history who recused all of the nonsense. I am reminded of Chesterton, who saw St. Francis as a man in love not with humanity, but with humans. Helen casts herself a grand misanthrope. Other people are soulless, unenlightened, unconscious, unaware morbidities, they add nothing to the progress of aesthetics. Love can be understood only by way of disgust, beauty by way of thin fingers. The musty smell of crypt is the glory of an artist's melancholy.

Just on the cusp of revelation, as always, the time has

come to depart, to leave the quiet and to resume the kinetic energy of outside. Only questions remain. Did the vision come despite the boredom, despite St. Francis's failure to materialize, despite knowing that the monastery life may not be exactly suitable after all?

These questions must be answered, but I have no time to answer them here. I must return to the world outside, perhaps I will have a moment of contemplation on the bus ride to Rome.

I leave the walls of the basilica, make my way with the others to the tour bus. Marieke tells us all she has a game planned for the rest of the journey, and those who would like to play should sit toward the front. I, for my part, have no interest in games at the moment, even though to play would be the chance to curry her favor, or even feel her eyes trained only on me for a moment.

Instead, I find my way to the very back, a place by the window, put my knees on the seat in front of me, set out to understand why boredom decided to sully the meeting of a saint.

THE BUS STARTS off toward Rome, our last destination on the tour, the last hotel room, last long bus ride to a new city, the time for Assisi has passed and I have exactly until the moment we arrive in Rome to figure it all out.

I pull out a tiny memo pad notebook, battered from the trip, attempt concentrated thought. I am distracted to the point of infuriation by the others on the tour, bodies propped with heaves into sagging bus seats for a game in which they must match artists to their philosophies. They then proceed to debate those philosophies entirely out of context, vulgar. Their putrid attempts at intelligence are pustules of excrement, dark ravages, each breath a witness to regret exited on another body. Even their skin crawls at the sound of their own voices. Marieke cannot possibly be interested in these people.

Yet she engages. Her long hair brushes against her breast, that must be the story. Yes, the story, and not her. She is merely a bookstore refund, an unwise epigraph, her words a swollen unnecessary prologue, central and marginalized, statement and annotation. She could easily be someone else and still the story would hold tight. Yet here she is. She has entered the story willingly, unconsciously, she must now be the character that finishes the story out. The story will end in time. If Marcel were here, he would write a good ending. His next plot point would be unexpected and perfectly calibrated. Helen's will be calibrated less perfectly, but the story must be as it is. Rome will design the conclusion, but first I must figure out the precise distance between me and the patchwork robe of St. Francis.

I sink down into the seat, the landscape rushes past as I consider the curve of Marieke's neck under her new scarf. The triumph of a purchase on a cold afternoon, she removes it as if it has been hers always, such nonchalance, such comfort, as if I've been a fixture around her neck feeling every turn and swallow.

The world of Helen Bonaparte must now be observed. I write the sentence into my memo book. The life of Helen Bonaparte, must, now, be observed. It has been up to now, what. It will not come, the next thought. A life examined is no life at all. Who said that? The nuisance of years.

I thought Assisi would be transformative. Let's consider why it was not. Why it was empty as an unbuttoned coat, a pristine top hat given over to a doomed sailor, unsatisfying and absurd.

The artistic impulse of a sainted figure is no more right or sane than any other. The defiance of uniformity achieved by stepping into a uniform. Perhaps poverty, then, unlocks the other mysteries, the ones I haven't been able to find, perhaps rejection is where art rises up, places itself on the bookshelf next to Marieke. Poverty, poverty. A university teaching position is hardly poverty. Perhaps St. Francis offered a revelation after all. A life without sentences written by students. Get one of those jobs at the bookstore. Just a part-time job, see what happens. But what about the children? Won't they suffer? Rationalize, Helen. Rationalize. Simple. No extravagant purchases, none of those and we should be fine.

All these thoughts are beginning to bore Helen, this lengthy detail on the way to Rome. Marieke chats with the Texan woman who knows nothing of buying scarves. I am impoverished by idiocy, poverty redefined as excess, nail-bitten moments lost in paperwork. Dull monotony, real life, too banal for today, for Assisi and for Rome.

These thoughts and their origins, painted canvas to blank one, words to their absence. Creation begets not creation, like the paradox in Beckett's Not Film. Creation, destruction, art, murder, factors in an equation that equals my glance to the front of the bus. She, art, me, the destroyer and the destroyed. The end, the beginning, pure mathematics.

All of this algebra may become meaningless when I return home, but now the Italian countryside beckons me toward certainty. I write in this worn memo pad: 42 divided by infinity equals zero. The sum of Helen's years divided by all the energy of the universe equals absence. Helen, the absence, a set of possibilities. David started the pattern that led to zero, his endlessness is to blame. The infinite requires me to divide myself into more than forty-two, requires a new equation, a new sum. Helen must change the equation, re-figure crawling moments, sighs and desire to escape.

Perhaps the answer is religious observance. Perhaps it is Assisi after all, but I hadn't the math to make it real.

Time and I end up right back in front of St. Francis's tomb, the infinite burned in decayed flesh and bone. I scribble down furious words in my tiny memo pad, pages granite black strokes that tear and resist this stage of abstraction.

My tour mates laugh in the front of the bus while I contemplate the ways in which art can be worshipped as a god. First, one must renounce all that is not art, money, pursuits that defile communion, excise the unimproved. Poverty, the refusal to create. I am Helen, in a mythic realm empowered, jeweled and writing on paper.

Helen takes a vow of poverty next to a touristed Italian gas station. The vow will come to life in Rome, she promises, as she takes control of her worship, renounces all that renders her futile, she will murder to create and by creating, carry out an act of murder. Algebra refines itself down to a memory. Helen, the sad goddess, humbled by the smile of a passerby staring cigaretted into a camera.

The last pages of paper fall, the letters are all scratched. The alphabet, proud of her efforts, gives the letters a droll look. I turn my eye away, look out the window at the roadway down below, decide to save these abstractions for another day.

THE SKY IS just turning dark when we arrive at the hotel. Rome's winding streets in their tangled exuberance draw me into the romance of grey-scaled Italian noirs. Rome, tawdry dirtcorners, Mr. Ripley clean shaven and walking to the American Express.

The hotel is clean like they keep the street outside, modern corporate logos name the atmosphere. We all enter, wait for rooms to be arranged, keys distributed, Marieke to call our names. We find the bar area and imagine a life in which we're drinking by now. Florescent pink and orange cushions pass for chairs, and darkened streetlamps reveal Roman passersby heading for dinner or for home. My only consolation against the slick veneer are the room keys, which are actual keys that must be returned to the desk before stepping outside the hotel, assurance that some textual aesthetics have been preserved. A dozen stories fill my head, all of which include women straight out of the 1950s.

I travel two floors up the elevator to arrive at the end of the hall directly adjacent to the breakfast room. After delighting in the turn of a golden key, I lay on the bed with a vague sense of fatigue, turn on the television to see if they have French TV. They do. Another consolation. Rome understands.

The room, crusted over with beige paint and a marble countenance, so modern, assaults my sense of adventure, so I open my suitcase and try to decide what to wear for dinner. This may be an evening of triumph, so I must look the part. An unanticipated lament. If only I had packed slightly more items that were not my uniform. All I manage to uncover is a bright blue sweater.

I pull the sweater over my head as French news broadcasters remind me that events are, in fact, still happening in the world. The belly protrudes, denim pants harsh, unforgiving this evening. Perhaps I should just wear the uniform. Perhaps, though, the triumph is in the blue sweater, which might be worn despite the look of my mid-section. Even because of the look of my mid-section! No, Helen, that's simply not it. Wear the sweater if you must, but let's not pretend about it.

I must be brave, find a way to remember the power I felt just a few hours ago if I am to become the poverty-stricken artist from my imagination.

The marooned and greyed walls envelop my stuffed body as the doorknob makes a slight half turn under my fingers. The room calls me back to its embrace. I regard the closed shutters, look again for any cracks in the wall. For good measure, I make sure Marieke's scarf has not been discovered. There in my suitcase it rests, safe in this keyed hotel room, a holy relic, secure under dirty underwear.

As we all walk to dinner, Marieke looks back often to make sure we keep up with her quickened footsteps. Richard makes it clear he had suffered through the Renaissance to finally arrive in this ancient city. He must have been a gladiator in a past life. He tries to teach us a few Latin phrases along the way, but the café windows distract us, too full of life.

At the restaurant, we are escorted to a large room at the back of the building, full of grand family style tables and at least a dozen other tour groups. The manager greets Marieke, then rushes to another table full of guests. This place, a cafeteria full of big American bodies, cracks a delicious smile.

Richard and I sit next to the young girls in our group, he entertains them by ordering a Fanta. They call him FantaMan, and he repeats the name with guttural elaboration. The girls giggle while I offer a chuckle to show solidarity with his attempts.

Marieke sits at another table this evening. It's only fair, she says to us, since she sat with us last night. I understand her reasoning but still find her logic faulty. She did lots of things with that group today, so does she really think they'll be upset? And then I realize what must be transpiring. She has no need to curry my favor. She knows of my worship, knows that any tip to come from me was acquired ages ago in Venice. I take it as a point of pride. She works now on the undecided, gives them a reason to dig in their pockets for the cash equivalent to her sacrifice.

The rest of the meal is eaten in relative peace. Even the young girls are civil, and I begin to engage in conversation with Richard about grammar schools in

England during the 1960s. He tells me all about schoolboy corporal punishment, he smiles in front of the pain.

After we order our drinks, we learn that there is a set menu here. Marieke appears beside me, confirms that she has ordered us both vegetarian meals. Richard continues his story, the soup arrives. The venue renders my palate nervous. Marieke sits with her back to me, her long hair celebrates the small of her back.

She opens her mouth wide, takes her first bite. Now is my chance to connect beyond tour guide and patron. We unite in the taste of soup on our tongues, salt and spice down the throat, delicious. My third ecstatic spoonful accompanies Richard's second Fanta, I begin to tease him, and then see across the way a turn of the neck, eyes that seek my own, a white smile, slender thumbs up. I meet her smile with a noncommittal nod, I am not entirely sure it is all for me.

But then, there is her mouth, her words take the shape of Helen, no voice, only lips sounding out The soup is good, yes? She speaks to me from across the room, I must find an equivalent response. Clumsy, I return her thumbs up, a pathetic showing. A wink meets me now, a wink of her eye! She seeks approval with whispers all over the table.

The rest of the meal is spent staring at the back of her head, twists of long hair careening past her shoulders like the universe in the blink of an eye. She converses across the restaurant drinking wine and making several toasts to each person at her table. How many toasts do there need to be in one meal? How many times is she going to show me just the slightest angle of her profile and then brush her hair back over her shoulder? How many times will I hear the faint of her laugh across the room as it travels over other table sounds and voices to reach me? How dare she wink and then offer me nothing but the side of her face? It's adulterous and uncanny, her aptitude for a slight. Each minute renders her actions absurd, and increasingly mean spirited. Ache and anger, even my bones feel slighted, even the blood in my fingertips would chastise you if it could, Marieke.

My eyes turn down. Focus the eyes down so the tears don't show, Helen.

The ache or the anger, which is more powerful tonight? The ache, infinite in an imagined touch of her cheek, the fact of her green sweater, her tiny white shoes. Or the anger, which pulls at her shoes by force to expose their treachery, rips the green sweater off her long slender body, bites down fully on its threads to taste the accumulation of her body in its fibers. The ache or the anger, which will be pursued tonight? Which will compel the next move, the next plotted storyline that I will regale in a long narrative to Marcel?

My body goes stiff on the hard, wooden chair, wine tastes of paper in my mouth. In this moment, I think of the kids, toiling away at their own artistic endeavors, excited voices on the telephone, small arms that hold me tight when they are afraid. I think of my job at the university, to which I will return in just a few short days, my general disdain for students, their ineffectual sentences and slouching bodies. I think of the books piled in our small apartment, stacks read and unread, many penned by Marcel. And I think of the piano in the corner that I play on occasion, toys on the mottled floor, meals left uneaten, moss along the chimney. I think of Marcel's deep voice as he tells the kids a story or practices his standup comedy routine. Marcel, a loved body and two decades of monologue. Book pages turn, dust and worn carpet stain the living room floor, unclean sheets that hold the sweat of sleeping bodies.

The anger or the ache is the question I must answer, my eyes riven to the spot where Marieke had been sitting just a few minutes before.

Richard reshapes my predicament with his kind voice, calls me back to chairs tucked back under tables and shuffling feet out the door. Richard asks, Are you alright, Helen? My eyes dart toward him. I take up my glass, say, Oh yes, I was just lost in thought, that's all, just a bit lost. He says come along now. Marieke is waiting outside to escort us back to the hotel.

ON THE WALK back Richard and I decide to try out the hotel bar with a nightcap and some almost-end-of-trip conversation. Richard, an innocuous addition to Italy, kind, witty, always ready for a laugh or two.

The hotel door is heavy as we enter, I cling to my jacket as we make our way to the far side of the lobby where five empty stools hug tight to an unattended bar.

We ask the night counter attendant if we can use the bar area. He says, of course, circles around the counter to make our drinks. I order a vodka and cranberry juice, Richard an Old Fashioned. After a few laughs at the expense of the Texans, I ask Richard why he's on this ramshackle tour anyway. How did we all end up here, just here, on a cool Roman evening after the torn robes of Assisi? He tells me he takes one trip each year, finds a tour that seems interesting, signs up without asking too many questions of himself. He says he's always loved Italy, especially Roman Italy, but wanted to get a bit of Renaissance into the trip as well. I call him an adventurer, he laughs out a disagreement.

He changes the subject rather abruptly, asks me if I'm having a good time. I say yes, very much, especially Florence. He asks about Marieke as tour guide, whether I like her. I say, She's fantastic. He chortles, there have been better, he says, she doesn't know all the best discounts. I compel him to agree that her long blond hair makes up for the offense.

Simultaneously, an idea is handed to us over the bar. Marieke, where is she? Yes, she should join us. She'd enjoy a drink and a laugh, it's the thing to do for the evening.

I volunteer to knock at her hotel room door. Hotel room door, I say with a secret vigor. I'm glad to take the lead, I saw, excusing it all with an after all, might not be quite the same to have a sixty-year-old man knocking on her hotel room door after ten.

Richard laughs his agreement while my feet carry me off to Room 310. Four rooms down from my own. Before I knock, I sneak into my own room to assess the redness of my face, touch my hands to my head in the mirror, brush the lint from my pants. I fancy myself attractive with even-toned lipstick. The knock, it will be momentous for Helen's assertive knuckle, the opened door a miracle, the bloodied palms of St. Francis.

I take steps down the hall after closing my own door softly to preserve the quiet. There before her door, I hesitate, nerves swell inside my fingertips. If she says No, no bother, maybe she's too tired, it's to be expected. Possibilities justify themselves to me as I knock, calmly, with politesse. I praise my hand for its boldness of attack.

A vague rustling from behind the door, I consider immediate escape. The weight of wallpapered pastel, my lungs, footsteps, eyes caught in a gleam of light, Marieke, an open door. She asks if everything is okay. Oh yes, I say, shyness and the skin on my neck, entangled lovers.

I say, Richard and I are enjoying a drink down at the bar, we're hoping you could join us? It'd be more fun with you there. A compliment perfectly timed. It's still rather early, and we're in Rome, it may be our last chance for a gathering. Hesitancy. She looks at the bedside alarm clock and after a moment's hesitation, says simply, sure. Sounds fun. I'll meet you down in just a few minutes.

The triumph is complete. I, Helen Bonaparte, successfully used my hand and fist to knock on the door that leads to Marieke, she agreed to follow my lead this time, supreme maneuver to revise the roles, to see her in a light she guards herself against, to sit alongside her body on a barstool in Rome. I head back down to the bar where Richard is waiting, tell him the operation was a success. I think to myself, the light in her room has touched the skin of my face. I have seen the bed she will sleep on after sharing a drink with me.

Downstairs at the bar the conversation is raucous, Richard's gregarious voice, stentorian echoing across the room while Marieke drinks whiskey to show that she can. She has decided to enjoy herself tonight, she tells us, lets us in on trip secrets such as how she is paid extra to steer tourists to certain shops, about her apartment in Rome, how tempting it is to sleep there tonight but she is contractually required to stay in the hotel in case guests need any assistance.

Richard tells her about all the times he's been to Italy, that he dreams of retiring here though not in the city, how he wants a bright yellow sports car to drive down the Amalfi Coast like he's in a James Bond film. She becomes her own laughter after a couple of drinks. Her inhibitions are flawless and falling with every step, mine are as well but in the opposite direction.

She tells us she is cold. It *is* rather cold, I say, with an imperative that the heat in this room be adjusted. I almost ask the attendant to do so. I enjoy the sound of her thoughts that lead me almost to action. I stay largely quiet, though, ask her a few questions, tell her I love all the behind-the-scenes tour group gossip. She says it's not that glamourous, that she needs to find her real path in life sometime soon. She says again that she's cold, remarks that her sweater is just upstairs, that she's thinking to go get it.

Helen's brilliance comes to life with a drink in its hand. No, Marieke, let me go for you. You've done so much for all of us, stay here and have fun with Richard, I can pop into your room very quickly and get your sweater for you. It's no problem, really. She delights in my helpfulness, says well okay, describes the sweater hanging on the desk chair closest to the door. She reaches into her pant pocket, pulls out her hotel room key, hands it across the bar to me.

I TAKE THE walk slow all the way up the stairs, thinking about the level of precision required for the task at hand. Too many minutes away and she would wonder what's happening in her room, too few and I'd regret missing the chance. Calculated piracy quickens my pace, I reach her door, the gold key lets me inside.

Her small suitcase, tempting on the bed, calls to me, taunts me with open latches but a closed lid. There would be no way to get inside without being discovered. I run my hands over the case, fingers slip inside surreptitiously, the soft of her clothing owns me for a moment. I turn my head and see the sweater on the chair. It is time. It is time to leave this room. Yet still, I slip my arms gently through the sleeves, I must do so, I pull it over my back, wrap it around my waist. Marieke's green sweater hangs to the ground at my feet, she is tall and it hangs low, absurd, obnoxious to the ground.

I slip into the bathroom, look in the mirror, marvel at the triumph. I must get going soon, but now I see emblems of her bathroom ablutions before me, soap, makeup, toothpaste, toothbrush, used just recently. I pick up the toothbrush like a sacred object, place its bristles to my front teeth. Subtle, brilliant maneuver. My mouth, hers again, my body, her scent, my breath, her teeth.

I remove the sweater, place it on a dry section of the countertop. One final move to make. A hand, unbuttoned jeans, wetness drawn out from hiding. I caress my own soft scent along the toilet seat. Her skin, my touch, here, unknown, joined in an act of ecstasy. I indulge one last moment, imagine her hands all over herself in the low twilight of the room, she touches herself to the scent of me.

Quickly, one last look, make sure all is exactly as it was. I hurry back downstairs, sweater draped over my arm and there she is, alongside Richard, laughter in conversation. An immensity. She slips the green fabric over her body while I take my place at the bar. I place the key into her hand.

We stay another hour, have one more drink, talk about banalities like whether the health system in America will ever improve. The cold air feels like a light touch from outside the door.

Eventually, we return to our rooms, we each anticipate a Roman morning. The two of us walk by her door, say our goodbyes. She tells me that Rome is her favorite part of the tour and she can't wait to show me the Sistine Chapel. I say there is no telling what may happen tomorrow. She closes her eyes as she smiles, turns her body toward her hotel room door.

My own room is hot with light and filled with the ongoing noise of the French news channel. I undress, lay uncovered in the bed, set the early alarm. I send a message to Marcel that I love him, missing him and the kids, starting to look forward to coming home. The lights get faint as I turn them out one by one, finally only the slow dim lamp at the bedside. I read a few sentences of *Those Who Walk Away* and fall deep into a silent sleep.

Day Six
Rome

THE SUN HAS taken its place on the stage of Italy, the manipulative sun, it fools us all into forgetting our jackets when we leave the hotel for the day. The breakfast room, as it turns out, is just next to my hotel room. Every footfall passes directly before my door to reach for lukewarm pots of coffee. I sit alone this morning, purposefully, at a tiny table, the sound of my thoughts my only company, the smell of mint on my breath noticed by no one except me.

I decide to let go of the uniform again today, opting instead for a longer black and grey sweater that hides the belly and makes no problem for the length of my thighs. The choice is well made come what may, with jacket or without, with shoulder bag or new leather purse.

The morning routine of rote decisions has forgiven me something today, though I cannot be sure what. Nonetheless, this morning was easy, readied me for a splendidly ordinary day. I must look the part of the jovial artist today, see if I can get a word out of my mouth to one of the large plastic women.

Breakfast ends with sweet jam and a cup of coffee. I head back to my room, just adjacent, to make final preparations for the day. Marieke's absence thus far allows paranoia a little tease, a slight cringe, a quick review of those few minutes. There could have been no outward signs of tampering. She must be attending to tour business, likely she ate early, Rome must be a nightmare to arrange, or maybe she went back to her apartment after all or met up with some Italian friends since she's in town. The reasonable explanation must have nothing to do with Helen. However, the change of pattern is conspicuous just after the events of yesterday evening. Best to play it safe today, best not to draw attention. Stay rooted in the background, Helen. Allow your black and grey stripes to smother you in their embrace, disappear into a smallness, regard the Vatican in silence, no comment, no question.

Small scarf tight around my neck, shoulder bag in place, raincoat draped over the arm, I cross the door's threshold just at the moment of a memory, a texture, silk to the point of a smile, her suitcase just there so innocent of my hands, so near her pillow.

Before I leave, I send a message to Marcel, tell him I will relate my adventures in the Sistine Chapel later this afternoon. I have such a story to tell when I return. I must write it down someday to show him the extent of my artistry. I must make him blindly jealous with my words, he must fully understand the extent to which his obsession with me should take root, take primacy, subsume his own artistic ambitions, his art in service of the self-awareness I will embrace on my return.

I task myself with walking as quietly as possible down the hall. She must be in the lobby downstairs. Remember, do not look at her at all today, not even a glance in her direction, not even while she narrates some fact of Roman history. My eyes must sink to themselves, look at my own reflection in windows, turn inward, Helen for your own safety on a day such as this, on a day when her ankles and morning oranges have been concealed from you, when you have not yet seen, though she has been awake at least an hour, the grey and blue scarf around her neck.

Marieke is downstairs, nonchalant at the front desk, reminding us all to turn in our keys for the day. The agent takes each one with an open palm and hangs them on their designated hook, a hook for every room, like the Atwood poem. I remark this fact aloud as I am compelled into uninterested Roman streets.

Marieke leads us down a few blocks to the underground subway, which we will take to the Vatican this morning. We are instructed to stay very close together. If we get separated, we are to exit on the platform marked something or other, I couldn't quite hear, she talks on and on as if we were toddlers and she the overexcited mother on a park bench full of strangers.

We board the train and its tracks leave us speechless. We immediately feel the teenager who finds the forbidden and doesn't care who sees. The subway ride exciting, dangerous, absurd, her hands almost at my throat. We did almost lose her, she was right to warn us, the mass of rushed bodies unaware of what they portend. I remind myself I am not here to judge only to journey.

The Vatican is somewhat disheveled and needing Marieke's guidance. We navigate the streets that surround the outer walls. The architecture asks, Are you alright, You don't seem well, my friend. Our polite small talk moves the moment around.

At the entrance we meet our new tour guide for the day, Lucia, another long green-jacketed distraction. I decide to ask her about it when we are out of the cathedral. Her jacket hangs past her knees, she smiles at me while she hands out the headsets. She, my pre-occupied today. Maybe I will touch her jacket, let nothing escape. My own body wishes to look that well-placed in a fitted long jacket, instead a bulging belly and oversized thighs hold moral clarity. I don't know at this moment whether I would like to be Marieke, or whether I simply want to be near her. I glance quickly as she tries to figure out a way to cover her belt.

I think of Marcel at home, likely asleep, wonder if he could handle the story of two women who will only ever meet again in the vigorous interactions of Helen's left wrist. Luckily, Lucia's green jacket has punk rock patches all over it, they will escort me through Roman artifacts.

Modernity assaults the entryway to the Vatican museum, assaults all the ancient things Helen imagines in every column, every relief, every broken tabletop, every worn carpet. Helen's angular tantrum is evident in crisp white columns, machines that test for metal, ticket booths, water fountains, tiny shops, tour groups with guides gasping into the audio headset. Here Michelangelo lay next to a tragedy of angles, mutilations of brush stroke, exertions of manipulative power over the lines of architectural progress. I sit on a side corner of the gaping entry waiting with the others for Lucia and Marieke to obtain our tickets. Tickets here sound absurd as gold slippers or a bag of silver coins, an outright blasphemy. Voices echo in capricious space, absurd with human voice, angry in its demand for silence, suffering noise that repeats all night even when the interior lay dormant and cavernous, nothing in its belly.

Helen is swallowed up here and now, the gullet of the

modern chokes her down its throat. I long for a novel by Thomas Hardy, Tess's long slow walks, miles of heather and crags. The Vatican swallows me down, spits me out on the other side of the entry way, wet and swollen and bruised and battered and ready for a call of Onward.

Looking for a way out, I hear Lucia's deep throaty voice scratching my ears about the age of the marble used in many of the statues that surround us outside. We have moved into a series of art-engorged rooms designed to overwhelm the aesthetic, rooms that breathe fire down the back and draw tears in their sheer voluminous pedigree. One fine sculpture after another informs my own dull capacity for creation.

We finally get through the maze of rooms, walk outside to the sidewalk entrance of the Sistine Chapel. A faded yellow signboard displays deteriorated images, details of the paintings we will encounter inside. The plastic covering over the signs are decayed to the point of crumbling, but Lucia pays no attention. She makes a few unremembered comments from the side of her mouth about the ceiling, tells us that none of what she can tell us matters compared to the experience of simply looking up. Simply looking up. I find myself ready for it. I am also intrigued by the dark color of her jacket as she explains that inside the chapel, we must be completely silent, an added notation we all accept as hyperbole.

As we enter, several guards shout a unison Silence! She was right, that Lucia.

Tourists huddle in groups looking at instructional guides, their vacant dispositions astound. I stand for a moment inside the cavernous belly of the chapel, remind myself that breathing isn't optional, hold tight to the bag around my shoulder. All the benches on the sides of the chapel are taken, so I stand in the direct center, head rested all the way back on my neck, gaping in fantasy, relief. My jaw begins to ache already in the first few panels.

The supposed silence retains a multitude of voices as the guards again intervene. I wonder about all these people from all over the world, what will happen to them when the ceiling comes crashing down in a wild ecstasy of Helen? What will happen to all of them when the figures above reveal their bare arms to me, when the men and women rejoice in the quality of my presence, when they remove their rosaries just for me, and they and I are one in a space just above the final lunette, when they look to me in surrender and contemplation, when they remove the mocking sashes over their genitals and ask me to remove mine as well, when they ask me to remain, to take my place as painted figure on well-worn wall?

Lucia told us just before entering to look at the progression of images as we walk through the chapel, that the artist learns his craft as he goes. The notion of imperfection is unimaginable, yet still I look for evidence. As I look down the panels, the cold story reveals itself. The initial image is indeed somewhat flat, almost merciless in its lack of detail, air flayed without muscle, figures formed with little definition other than religious narrative. The next panels become more defined, more egregious in readings of their own narratives, and by the end the arms, the arms tangled and reaching toward each other, the arms, they reach out, grasp into the blue air, the arms, they reach down around me, the figures they cannot stay affixed, they must descend down to the earth, they are not of the heavens, they are fully of the earth, these last paintings that reach out of the sky to touch an unknown and unforgiving world, they are of the artist alone, they are for the artist, the man who conceived and used his hands to create, they become the masterpiece that is not for heaven, not for god, not for angels, not for saints, but for the artist who touched the earth and skin and reached out for another man's skin and legs and chest and arms and hair. He saw in the male human form a dire revelation, a corporeal groan, a desire fused with art that brought a body close to his. In David he carved the rude body all for himself, and here he refused to clothe these male forms, no need to shield them from his crisp eyes, they are the artist himself giving them a holy meaning and an aching forlorn desire. Here the artist's hands all over the flesh, the artist fusing himself into his subjects, bringing them into full flesh, a brush full of flesh and a scent wrapped around their genitals. Michelangelo walks down the chapel ceiling toward me and tells me, yes, you have the right and yes, poverty is all it is meant to be, yes, you must learn to wrap flesh into your flesh, all flesh, her flesh, and all flesh must become you all over, you and the savior and the martyr, you are the saint who saves the world from itself, you, the artist, are the one who gives them all meaning and a purpose and a form that will render them immortal, you, yes, Helen of Assisi will serve the work by sacrifice, by creation, the act of daring forth, the world in your pen and paper, you will render the world purposeful just like me, he says, and these smears and lines of myself are there to tell the story not of the bible, but of the religious symbolism of art itself. He says, here I am with you in the eternal orgy of creation, I descend upon you with willing hand to guide you through the crucifixion, the rejection, the turmoil, the failure, as you learn your own recklessness, your own flesh drawn according to your own selfish desires.

I AM CARRIED by colors and faded silks to the back of the chapel. I wait for the others to pass through. I glance up to see one of the lunettes that looks conspicuously like an image of a seated man looking back on the paintings all along the chapel, looking back over his shoulder to judgment day, to god and Adam, to the men in their aching flesh and to the women's breasts. I see

Lucia there near me, ask her the meaning of that one image.

She tells me, Some have speculated it is a portrait of the artist surveying his work. I respond, Of course! Of course it is Michelangelo himself regarding all he created, artist as god, as deity, as creator. He paints himself facing forward, toward the future, toward the next work, the next flesh in his hands, the next step toward despair and perfection. He faces forward, but turns only his head, cranes only his eyes back just to take one last eternal look, yes that look back, that cracking open of the spine just to see the words in print, that gentle caress of the sculptor's hand as the next block of marble is unshelved into an arm, the last brush stroke, that eye that stares out just as he says It's done, the enthused fascination at the feat he has accomplished, the murder of art, the murder of the artist is the head turning away a final time, the birth and death of art is in the head turned just that way, the book closed and put on the shelf as you open another empty notebook. Of course the artist paints himself there. Looking back forever. The chapel and the artist formed and unformed.

The learning of the panels, the touch of creator, the head of Michelangelo turned back, his eyes are in the face of god, his brushstroke in the outstretched hand of Adam.

I tell Lucia, Of course it is the artist.

The course of my own history is simply the artist looking back, murdering to create, murdering absence, murdering the blank canvas, the blank page, perpetual envy of what will fill the pages, beauty, or failure, the lure of a woman's breast, or the footfalls we hear in the night in a film by Bresson.

I am birthed out of the chapel in an ecstasy, then thrust into the empty square, hollow in its collection of tourists who have looked but not seen a miracle, who pass through eternity without stopping to gather the point of origin, a hand held to the chin in contemplation.

The square outside St. Peter's gives us all a necessary infusion of wide open arms, of space the size of vistas that look on the apartment of the pope while we stand uninformed of a millennia of abuses that have likely taken place at just this spot.

I am still aching with the portrait of the artist, still

burning solid. Fixed in form, my head turns to look around for Marieke. I see her there in her short blue skirt, and I am suddenly an absurdity. I have been found. She has found me only to escort me into future silences. The long, loving, empty square trails off in a thousand directions. Silence as solid as Vatican walls. Silence alongside sound, both at once, stillness and communal sighs, beauty and the smell of exhaust fumes.

We lean in for a few minutes while we all catch a breath, the Texans moan on about Michelangelo as if they have any idea what the portrait means, how the world has changed. These fellow tourists are less intrigued by art itself than I understand, and I am sure the fat man has eyes for me. There is no dust in his eyes as they rest on me.

The square is empty, and it makes me feel empty too, all except my fingernails which may simply be uninterested. We turn, follow Lucia's lead. I make sure Marieke is supplementary, at the rear of the line. We enter St. Peter's massive, dark cathedral, gold-stained glass and knaves at all ends, the glory of god seen from all directions here in the grandeur of well-rendered space.

Eventually, every congregant must turn her eyes away to view the work of the artist.

We stand and gape. I stand and gape at the side of the church. Through the tour guide's speech, I pay no attention to who died here long ago, who was born a knot of shyness in a mother's yes. The dead body in the crypt, the priest and his nice to meet you, the organ pipes wonder. I cannot get interested in a church much longer. I have seen altars more profound than any pew, though still I must like everyone else take part in the touching of St. Peter's foot. The statue of him perches, looks over us all, his foot only a nub after so many hands. I walk before the foot, stand near the line but not in it, wait for a moment. Richard tells me I must, Marieke comes to me and asks why the hesitation. How can I tell her the danger she may be in?

A few quarter notes of persuasion compel me at last toward St. Peter. The graven solid image has taken an anthropological appearance, an amputation not yet wrapped in gauze. He is the inevitability of so many hands, even my own slick oils are now part of the deterioration. Profound desire. Intense despair.

Back at St. Peter's square, I look to the window where the Pope makes his proclamations. His are political more than aesthetic. I am an emissary, sent to tell you all I shall tell you all, in the room the women come and go buries itself into my subconscious, involuntary, Eliot's exact words travelling up into the Pope's chamber, grasping columns to land at my feet in humble sacrifice. Words sacrifice themselves to be given voice and sound and letter. Eliot was a murderer too, though he would be too prudish to admit it.

It turns out that even after my resolution not to speak today, I have a genuine question, one for a tour guide such as Lucia or Marieke. Either would do in this case, which indicates to me that my question is real and not simply a ruse. Here I think of returning to the comfortable state of things, of being survivor in some self-inflicted repetitive destruction.

For this question, Lucia would actually be preferable. She likely knows more about the subject. However, she is off catering to those tourists still lumping along in the basilica. My genuine question has to do with the open door of the church. I want to know what dates the church was built, how long construction continued before it was done. Michelangelo admittedly painted the ceiling of the establishment next door, and now Helen would like to place a question mark at the end of her sentence.

Lucia cannot be found, so I pose the question to Richard who stands just to the left checking the time on his phone. He tells me he couldn't possibly know a thing like that, points to Marieke with a nod. Ask Marieke, he seems to say. She would know, he says, the words with a beautiful innocence taken right from Blake's sonnets.

I tell him I couldn't possibly bother her, that it's no issue, I'd look it up later. He tells me that's nonsense, and his stentorian voice beckons her from across the square. Her cold hands and smile arrive in a matter of seconds. Yet I cannot find words. My early morning decision lingers in my jaw as I begin to form half of a question. I ask, stammer in words spoken backwards, she knits her brow in confusion.

I refuse to speak, vaguely upset that she and Richard have both been witness to the truth. Helen is being made the fool, just now, here where the Pope looks on.

Marieke finally understands the question, looks up at the church façade all the way to its spire and back down to its doors, says with frivolity, I really don't know.

Either Helen has found Marieke's only weakness, or else she is purposely withholding intonation as a punishment for the crime of desire. I cannot tell which is the truth. I mumble an It's okay, I'll look it up later, turn my face away toward the street sounds below. Richard and Marieke end the scene with some note about open hours of the Forum, concern that we may miss the last open minutes. I think fondly of St. Peter's foot, desired, worn to a shiny stub, all the fond hands have the pleasure of its touch.

AFTER WE LEAVE the Vatican City walls, the less civilized members of our tour group want to shop for Catholic-themed trinkets in a lane of shops just outside the city walls. Marieke tells them they have thirty minutes, that we need to eat lunch then catch the bus to the Coliseum. Shopping holds none of my interest. I have already purchased my relics, a purse and a postcard.

I wait outside the shops with Richard. Marieke steps

in our direction, uninvited, and places herself squarely into our conversation. I think, I am past age forty-two, these interruptions should no longer make my lips shut tight. Richard and Marieke speak about the colors of rosaries, about the Pope's face on a cheap t-shirt. I am still thinking of Michelangelo, such beauty and wit to be discussed but instead everyone wants to speak of doorknobs and decorations.

I decide the madness must end. I cannot fathom her contrived roil of banality, it must not be so. I speak to her while Richard looks away and enters a nearby shop. I can see him in the window. I ask, did you see Michelangelo's self-portrait looking back on the far side of the chapel? She takes my question literally, says Yes, she has heard that the panel is meant to reflect the artist. I recount an abbreviated form of my own conversion, tell her the portrait *is* the chapel, that it's all right there, the artist at the furthest reaches of possibility, of identity, of perfection. I realize the melodrama as I speak, but I continue. The evolution of the artist's style leads directly to him sitting there, reflecting on his work, surveying the meaning of all that intellectual and physical labor. She looks at me with two eye blinks and says calmly, with no sense of consequence, I tend to dislike when artists place themselves into their work, it steals something from the work, makes it about the artist rather than the subject.

Helen cannot contain her appalled disgust. She would have preferred not to have this information. Marieke, the student of art, a work of art herself in Helen's capable hands, does not understand. The subject? Never. Cowardice. Marieke, you have made a terrible mistake.

Helen glimpses the extent to which she fantasizes Marieke into intelligence. This woman's white teeth are more suited to the Texans than to me, no wonder she shares a drink with them while Helen revolts at another table. Helen is a single footstep out of step with itself, a cut whisker, a neckline with one conspicuous missing pearl. She is the crack she avoids on the sidewalk, the theatre spotlight turned to the wrong actor, the sound of a quarter dropped into a well just before the wish and not after.

Marieke veers off in one direction, Richard and I in another. We find a small restaurant with outdoor seating, we must eat before arriving in ancient Rome, the perfect meal, a bridge from the splendor of Michelangelo to the austere ruins of the gladiators.

Helen's word has become ancient now. The remainder of the trip will forego the Renaissance to focus instead on ruins the Renaissance artists plundered. The time for rebirth is over, now it is time for death.

A small restaurant waits for us just around the corner, alleyway filled with pedestrians. The prices are reasonable, so we sit down, wait to be served. The Italian waiter seems suppressed, or oppressed, or depressed, at any rate uninterested in serving us our meal.

There is nothing on the menu that seems particularly satisfying, so I order yet another slice of pizza and a peach iced tea. Both arrive, but my mouth has no taste. The bitter tea fills my mouth with disappointment. Richard talks about Roman gladiators, tells me about evolution of their armor over time. I am interested, but I also focus on the skin underneath my fingernails as they drum against the empty water glass.

We finally gather on a street corner to wait for the bus to the Coliseum, the street corner livid with envy and pink accents. My stomach feels taut with too much pizza as I lean quietly against a brick façade. I talk in subdued tones with Richard. He is excited for Coliseum revelry, I myself have had my fill of Rome.

The bus arrives, malingers, then rends its way through complicated streets. It drops us off among a mass of human bodies, sweating, aching to taste the ancient world. How can Helen be also a human being if this is what they look like? Helen doesn't feel of this world, of these people, of these streets and avenues. Put her back on the Bridge of Sighs, lock her up in an anchorite cell with only her mind to philosophize her condition. She will craft an ecstatic religious meaning out of a dirty mattress and a few quill pens.

We get in a long single file line to enter the Coliseum. There has been some complication, we missed our ticket entrance time. Marieke and Lucia flash their Italian and Dutch eyes, maybe slip the guard a few Euros, and eventually we are in. Our wait is over as we rise from our positions to the side of several garbage cans.

Inside, the structure is haunted by carcasses of killed lions, by enslaved men who were led here to their deaths, by the enthusiasm of spectators willing it all to happen. I cannot get enthusiastic about the ethics of the place, it's beyond what Helen is willing to endure. This murderous flatland, this protracted culture, this set of architectural decays that lay just beneath the surface of the world. It is not to be born of flesh and blood.

One of the younger girls stands next to me as I look out over the cells where men and animals were asked, Do you want to die? She tells me there is depressed beauty here. I feel the same way. Too much death collected, celebrated here, mutiny, gore, torture, cruelty.

She asks, Why do we celebrate this place?

I tell her that human beings are abominations and always will be, it's best for her to stay away from all of them if she can help it. She laughs, says she already tries her hardest, begins a long monologue about young despair, fatigue from the ugliness and cruelty and stupidity she sees every day. I tell her that I admire her insightfulness, then wonder if I did the right thing. Yet she is right. I would be lying if I told her to have a more positive outlook.

We agree that the Coliseum is a bust, turn to look for our tour group. They are nowhere, so we walk around the perimeter, on the lookout. They left us behind, our laughs are amused irony. Human beings aren't so bad when you need them for something.

Eventually, we track them down in the gift shop, give each other a nod of solidarity. Of course they are in the gift shop. I linger outside with Richard while young girls and Texans purchase magnets for their kitchens and dangling keychains laden with images of decay. They exit, at last, and we are off to the forum. Richard promises to give me a lesson in translating Latin.

THE GATE TO the Roman Forum secrets itself just down the street, an ancient relic, the Forum unknown to me. I hope to learn its significance. Do we revere it simply because the ruins are old, ravaged by Renaissance artists whom I admire terribly and in whom I can find no fault? These important places lay stoic and impressed, as if a tiny stone house that holds a single lonely artist is any less impressive.

Lucia and Marieke, our two Virgils. They arrive at the gate just as it is being closed and locked by some very insolent guards. The group is visibly upset at this turn of events. We have missed the Forum, after coming all the way from Texas, one woman drawls out of her crooked mouth. The girls type on their phones our misfortune.

Lucia's long green stylish jacket gets visibly irate as she gesticulates to the guards in Italian, grand waves of her hands and a gesture out to us. Something in her manner attracts and repels me, something in the scratch of her older voice makes her both song and scrawl. She must have a similar effect on these guards, who finally open the gates just to let us through, telling a few others who had gathered that they should come back tomorrow.

Once inside, the landmark's confusion amounts to moments spent deciphering where one building long ago stopped and another started. I look around for Richard to explain it, after all he grew up in England and has very good handwriting.

I finally catch sight of his bearded grey face across the ancient plaza. He is talking to the awful Texan woman who earlier this week I hoped would be caged naked in a public cell. He rolls his head back in laughter at something she says. I now question his mirth. He laughs indiscriminately.

Forget the Forum. It has been here a long time. More importantly, I lament that my day started with a portrait and is ending with a potted plant two thousand years old. It is an injustice of a day, carried intellectually from the pinnacle to the perimeter, the heights to the mildly amused, from perfection to ruin.

I wander around, eventually find a seat near to Lucia telling some members of the group about relics, government buildings, performances, all the daily lives these decayed stone forms represent. I sit and listen on behalf of her jacket, fortunate to be attached to such a small frame. I listen also for the sake of her voice, which travels optionally through audio headphones. I prefer the quiet, carved out into the unforgiving wind, the sound of her voice fading quickly as she speaks each word.

It is getting dark, and it is time to leave. The day has been a gamble, a bated breath. I can't wait to leave this place. Ruins this ancient offer no satisfaction, no solace, no spirit of the artist who fends off decay for just a few minutes longer. Richard gains great satisfaction from decay, I admire him for it. Helen needs the vibrant, the inward, to feel fully herself.

We leave the Forum, head back to the hotel by train, and prepare ourselves for dinner. Our penultimate dinner in Italy, let's see where Marieke sits tonight. It is according to her logic, "my turn," since she has been dallying with the Texans for the past two nights. We are due for a glass of wine, she says while I envision her long hair spilling across the table. I shall wear my habit, an act of defiance against my own imaginative whims.

When we arrive at dinner, we are escorted to a tiny back room just large enough for our tour group of twelve. The restaurant seems the exactitude of a quaint, side-street Italian meal, the kind of place where houses and shops commingle in secret, a story's perfect start, intrigue, broken promises, shattered glass, a hand extended out in surrender.

I watch as the patrons take their seats. Marieke ushers them to comfort and a sense of security. She speaks Italian with the restaurant staff, perhaps ordering us a vegetarian meal. She laughs at the man, he has said something to make her laugh. Was it an actual witticism, or is she simply being her version of kind, a treacherous dishonesty, an ugly taunt of suffocation?

She looks around. I have taken my seat in calm delight, ignoring her presence. After a moment and a poured glass of wine, she takes her seat at the end of the table, the head of the table, right next to me. Our legs almost touch under the tablecloth. She has come to me tonight, unknowing and brilliant in her decision.

I am careful not to seem too enthusiastic, even though we did share a drink yesterday evening. She must not suspect my intentions, even now after several days of unchained encounters. I am unmistakably brilliant in my performance. We chat about the Coliseum, about almost getting lost, about the incident at the Forum gates. Others join our small talk as we wait for our meal.

When the food arrives, we share another disappointment together. After an appetizer of cheese and bread, we are served a caprese salad for dinner, overripe tomatoes to the side of more cheese. We look to the side at each other in an unspoken solidarity of quick-witted condemnation and hunger. Two smiles break through the silence as we pick up our forks to swallow down the meal.

We talk about time, and restlessness. Her desire to

find meaning in some occupational outlet. Her decision to go back to her Dutch home, stay with her parents a while, figure out what to do with a Master's degree in Art History. I fine-tune my enthusiasm, play cheerleader, the one who sees her capacity for beauty. We discuss the passage of time, the oddity of our ages. I say I am ready to make a complete and total life change. She tells me she is in the same position.

The question becomes the decision, we agree. We reminisce about things we never shared, frustrations, detached necessities that implicate the purest of pursuits. We tell our stories, trajectories that become intensely destructive. We toast several times to our paths' convergence, our similarities, small things alongside the vastness of several pieces of cheese still left to consume.

They bring out dessert menus. We toast to dessert. We toast to Richard. We toast to the candle having gone out at the table. We toast to Rome and to Michelangelo. We toast to the tapping of our shoes to each other's accidentally under the table.

We bring each other into our shared conversations to feign nonchalance. We prove to everyone at the table that Marieke is here not only for me.

Marieke is here only for me.

I consider whether to rekindle our earlier conversation about time and restlessness, but I choose to let it go. She convenes with slow fingers on wine glasses, tongue to lips, talk of the wonders of Italy.

Our conversation tapers into windy roads of nowhere, a brief remark here or there but none given especially to me. I know she must do her job, which is not solely conversing with Helen Bonaparte in the corner of the restaurant, but there are moments she takes it a bit too far. Helen is left sitting without referent, without story, trapped in someone else's composition book.

It is time to excuse myself to the restroom, which I am not embarrassed to do since no one is paying attention. I whisper a polite, unheard excuse me, head across the room and down the stairs to the lower level of the restaurant. The strange offers its surprise even as I begin to descend. Along the wall of the stairwell are hung several American-style Halloween decorations. Someone is enamored with witches of all sorts, cute, happy witches, witches carved out of wood, witches decorated with paint and ribbons of orange and purple. One witch is on a broom, another stands next to a spooky tree, one sits alongside her black cat. As I descend even deeper toward the restroom, the stairway opens to a rather large sitting room just outside the bathroom door. The room is filled with more witches, some purposefully scary, dark red eyes and turned eyebrows, others rather cheery, as if waiting to bake a set of gingerbread curlicues. Some sit on horses, stuffed with straw and cotton, some lay within a den of fake spider webs on a long table, dozens and dozens of witches, all seemingly plundered from Halloween superstore overstock at a discount, or from some Roman specialty store that deals in American kitsch.

The bathroom is straight ahead. I make my way there, thankful to be leaving the witch room. Only one solitary witch haunts the toilet, a happy one. I don't dare take my eyes off her for a second while I urinate.

The witch ordeal having come to a close, I quickly ascend the stairs to join the gossip again, oddly feeling safe among the new familiar faces. I sit down and see Marieke standing at the other end of the table, not eyeing me, but engaged again in a jovial conversation with one of the Texans. No bother, at least I am out from the witch's den. I tell Richard he must see the restroom level even if only to admire the décor.

Marieke is standing closer to me now, nearer to the table. She mentions the Spanish Steps, says it's a shame we won't get to see them on the tour, it's one of her favorite places in Rome. I make my voice heard though she wasn't speaking to me, tell her I'm disappointed as well, that I've always wanted to see the Spanish Steps where Keats expired and where certain scenes from Patricia Highsmith novels take place.

She looks at me directly and says, with uptilt to her voice, well, let's go then. Tonight.

She said let's go then, tonight.

I can take you there. It's only a 20 minute walk from the hotel.

I peer out my slight Okay, surprise measures my voice, that would be fun, yes, let's.

The plan is set. Once we return to the hotel, we two will walk alone for twenty minutes to the Spanish Steps.

My name is Helen Bonaparte. Have I mentioned I am a goddess?

My steps are orange like the walls I walk between. I must not make any move that would change the course of the evening, the color of the Spanish Steps reveals itself to me slowly as I move toward the door. We will first walk back to the hotel to deposit the others, then we will leave the hotel to walk to the steps together, only our two bodies will breathe Roman air, our eyes will drink in the same sights.

As we leave the restaurant, several members of the group begin shouting expletives in the street, all drunken musicality but an embarrassment nonetheless. Marieke attempts a soft phrase, Let's stay quieter here in the residential area, but two young girls and the Texan who was not crying at Dante do not listen.

I ache to possess the kinetic power to shove their full bodies hard against one of these crumbling brick walls, to see, if nothing else comes of it, the look of horrible surprise on their faces as their feet leave the ground unexpectedly. They belch unintelligible words out into the night air, words with no referent or hygienic purpose, no meaning other than inebriation to the point of ugliness.

I wish for Marieke's sake I could stop them. Instead, I think about the Spanish Steps where Keats wrote a poem long ago.

We arrive at a bus stop that Marieke thinks will be much quicker than walking. She tells us to wait for the next bus to arrive.

I wait in a circle of strangers, use Richard as my guide for when to add my own voice into the mix. The talk is of nothing, rememberless droning, that sound of wishes and stones.

The bus arrives, as predicted, a bulging mass of people inside, inordinately full so that some of our group must stay behind. Marieke remains on the corner with them, says they will catch the next bus. I am ushered onto this one unwillingly.

The bus separation will foul my plans, in all probability, she will lose her willingness after such a stressful return to the hotel. I sit on the bus in the only free seat while the rest of my tour mates stand. I don't care if they are older or fatter right now. I pull my loneliness up to my chest in adolescent angst, in jealousy, in hope and in the feeling that the universe has gone square against me.

Perhaps the woman was right, the one who jumped out the window in Assisi.

We arrive on the corner a few blocks from the hotel, grateful Richard knows where we are, mill around, regard shop windows and subway tracks across the dark night. We wait for Marieke to arrive on the next bus. Though the group's conversation seems innocuous, I speak to no one. I have no need for mild chatter from such a random allocation of people.

At last the second bus arrives, we all walk together to the hotel. I wait for Marieke's confirmation that the date is still on, that she wasn't merely speaking out of her mouth. I dare not say a word about it first, desperation may be interpreted when really there is merely fascination. How shall the walk be written? How many slightly worn faces will we see under the lights of a Roman sky? And will we speak of them?

She shows her own desperation while I pass through the hotel door. She holds it open for me, says a quick See you in ten minutes here in the lobby. I nod, surreptitious, head to my room to fashion the look on my face. Best not to change clothes, certainly. Eight minutes later arrives, I check my distended belly for the last time. The door ushers me out into the hall with an air of nonchalance.

SHE WAITS FOR me while looking at a map of the area given away free by hotel management. I walk to her, full breath held in my mouth, see the lights from outside the window turn her long hair translucent. I say, Are we ready? She says, let's wait another few minutes, and continues, I invited Darlene to walk with us, she told me on the bus that she was also sad to miss the Spanish Steps.

Darlene. Darlene. Who is this Darlene? Another tour patron, yes, but which one? I fraction in my attempt to place the name with a person's voice. I fail miserably. One of the young girls? One of the nondescript few I have had no thoughts about one way or another? Darlene, an impossible task.

I say, Oh okay simultaneously with the appearance of Darlene, cumbersome around the corner. Darlene, the high school teacher Texan who fake cried at Dante's tomb. Darlene, the woman who made a ridiculous classroom puzzle from David's postcard body. Darlene, whose large white fingers upbraid my conscious self. Darlene, loud voice shouting across the plaza, Darlene with a book in her hand she does not know how to read, Darlene who will likely tell us her opinion of Keats as a lame high school lesson plan. There are few words that can capture my indignation and betrayal, a deflation Helen will suffer all evening. My heavy steps, Marieke's ear turned toward the woman's lipstick breath. Her greasy fingerprints inflict suffering on the window glass as she exits the hotel.

Her residue haunts me as I follow behind.

Helen is a cut chord ringing out its eulogy to the sound of the synthesizer. Helen is cobbled together footsteps littering the ground with ash. Helen is a ponytail pulled too tight, a cat's paw drowned in blood, roaring sharp claws. Helen is throttle and lazy evidence all over the living room floor.

The walk to the Steps, the long, slow, painful walk to the steps where Keats drew his last breath 300 years ago, the walk was planning its revenge.

Marieke and the Texan tell a loud story to each other. Marieke laughs when the woman points out a half-dressed mannequin, and she laughs when the woman recounts a mispronunciation of Inferno. The woman pulls her own hair into a short barrette to monopolize attention.

Marieke tries to draw me into the conversation by reminiscing about our day at the Colosseum. I chime in for a moment, say I was more impressed with Michelangelo's self-portrait, but the two only nod peremptorily. We three walk. I stay a footstep or two behind to glare and bellow out my silent ire at the jacket pleats in front of me.

We finally arrive. We stand at the bottom of the steps looking up.

They marvel, I scowl. They speak of memory, I speak of death.

The Texan's mouth irons out the word Keats, and at that I have had enough. Her scratching at the inside of my eardrum gives me over to ugly thoughts. I wish there were nothing like consequences, only those save her now.

I hear across the way a teenage boy calling out for his brother. I see the house where Keats composed and died. I feel nothing, I cannot get my mind back to its origins. The stone has been thrown and it's much too big. I cannot get my mind to ponder Keats right now, my plan has not yet been composed. Composed. Composure. Composing. Composition. Decomposition. Decompose. I must decompose these scenes of Steps, each one upward a note of revenge so that Helen will know that kind of power.

I want to fling myself against the cement wall in a rapturous, triumphant shout, but to do so would draw suspicion. About this time, though, I realize I have formulated the perfect plan.

I hear the other two voices become less compelling as they travel back toward me. This woman, she is a moment killer, a person who likely opens her daughter's journals without asking, who swats a fly at its sound of gasping breath. To leave the top of the steps so quickly, I'd bet she's never even heard of Glenn Gould.

I climb myself now that they have come down. I ready myself for the return walk while looking down at them from the top step. I glance over to see the Keats house just for memory's sake, tell myself I must capture a picture before we turn to leave. The two of them continue their descent together and I cannot decide whom to disparage more acutely. Their jackets are almost the same color green, mine is deep black. They both have yellow hair, mine is red. They will both cauterize here in Helen's memory like the picture of Keats' death bed.

The walk back to the hotel is a burden of lust and empty hands. We go quickly as Marieke worries about being away from the hotel for too long. She attempts to engage me in conversation, I oblige but only with sullen eyes. I tell her and the Texan standing beside her about my university teaching position and the work I had to do to get it. I tell them I'm excellent at carrying a plan to fruition even if it means burning the rest of life to the ground.

I am silent after that, polite and silent as a sleeping cat. Once we arrive, I return to my room and curl into bed, staring with blank eyes at a French crime drama I only half understand.

Day Seven
Pompeii

THE LAST DAY of the tour and what is Helen doing? Helen is in her hotel room after a long night's sleep. She is rough and tumble along a dirt path, she is the underside of a cat's belly, she is the mind that orders soft drinks at midnight because fuck losing weight, she'll be Gertrude Stein instead of Djuna Barnes, her body the breaking point, disabused and unattractive, she her own defense against the tyranny of desire.

Helen stands before the mirror regarding her face, making sure facial hair remains unnoticeable. She stretches out the skin around her lips to feign an unwrinkled smile, noting the crease in her chin that has taken hold over years of laughter with Marcel.

She takes stock, asks herself if the trip has thus far been a success. Ultimately, she cannot decide, but is sure to have an answer by the evening. The answer will be as amorphous as answers always. She is Falstaff today. That which I am, I must be.

Helen brushes her teeth over a sink of running water. The task is a forlorn part of her day, with its air of responsibility and ruthless necessity. These daily ablutions have always cost Helen a great deal. Her time, her hour of what to wear, her daily miscalculations, her intoxication of anxiety before walking out the door.

The faux marble sink stares at her face as she drowns out the sound of the overhead fan with her thoughts. What was the purpose of this trip? Has the goal been achieved? Are there truly activities in life meant merely for one's enjoyment, no higher purpose than that? Helen agrees with herself. The light switch turned to off confirms that the proposition is absurd and untimely.

The morning routine almost lulls her back to her senses, back into the warm sound of Marcel. He has called a few times to no response. He wants to make sure all is well, to see how I like Rome. I must return his call at some point, but the uninteresting drowns me out, I feel boring, no tales to relate, a true lack of flavor. I must have a story to tell, to keep the spirits positive, must find the angle that will intrigue him enough for my own satisfaction. Yet the trip has been ultimately uneventful, though I myself have been having a spectacular time. Marieke, the vista of my waking eye, the consideration of my daily wardrobe.

I exit my room door, rapid pulse, the shadow of my wrist haunting the shape of my body. Our last breakfast of the tour. The dining tables just adjacent, I will walk into the room with a breath full in my lungs. I will reveal the blue shirt I am wearing with blue jeans and black shoes laced all the way up. I will not care where I sit, I will sit alone or not alone, I will sit as far away from her as I can.

My feet square their way into the room just as panic sets in over the orange juice maker. The tables are all full, Marieke is nowhere in the room, the coffee pot waits to be refilled. I ask myself again what I had hoped to accomplish and cannot remember a single possibility.

Richard reposes at the other end of the dining room with two women I had never seen. These two are just gathering their belongings to leave, so Richard tags me with a wave of the hand, motions for me to sit down and join him. I gather some food, lukewarm oatmeal and an orange, take a place across from him as he narrates previous visits to Pompeii. The dining room, opaque in its banality, has given over to corporate art and pink highlights. I search the room, find the Texan woman's voice, hear the words Spanish Steps.

My attention must stay on Richard's tale for it will inform my enjoyment of the day. The coffee pot waits for Marieke's hands. Yet how could she enter after last night's betrayal? It is impossible given my resolution not to let it go unpunished. I remember the crime drama on television last night, corpse with bloodied hand attempting to ward off a lover overcome with jealous rage. The Texan begins to stuff her mouth with prepared animal flesh, sacrificed so she might expand herself on a Roman street with Marieke's scarf two feet away from her creped neck.

A well-dressed woman interrupts my loathing. She is

a front desk attendant, she announces, perusing tables for someone in Marieke's party. She questions the table across from us, they say No. Richard and I decide to speak up, we're with Marieke, we say. Intrigued, my thoughts turn to last night in the hotel lobby as Marieke looked back to me once before returning to her room.

This woman holds out a package, tells us it includes items for several people in Marieke's tour group, items purchased yesterday from stores that slated them for delivery today. Ah yes, I say, I remember those items. I was there at the purchase, yes, I remember who bought them. Yes, I will gladly deliver the package to Marieke. I thank her for the trip all the way up to the breakfast room, Grazie and Ciao and so on.

Richard asks what's in the packages. I tell him I have no idea, that I was lying just to be able to deliver the package myself to Marieke. He chuckles, tells me I'm strange. I tell him I couldn't agree more. An enthusiastic 'I couldn't agree more' leaves my throat, exclaimed with Martha's inflection from *Who's Afraid of Virginia Woolf.* The reference goes unnoticed. Only Marcel shares these endless, in-referenced moments, intimate, timeless, brilliant.

I wonder now, what shall I do with the packages? I haven't bothered to learn a single person's name, other than my British friend and the Dutch tour guide, who is, after last night, unknown to me. I ask Richard what we should do with the box. Laugh. Deliver it to Marieke! After all, her name is on the outside. I tell him that really was my plan all along anyway. He smiles wide, says Okay, as if speaking in a foreign tongue all the way from home.

Marieke arrives just as I drink my last sip of coffee, her entrance planned just so. She herds us all downstairs to start the bus ride to Pompeii, tells us we must be on time.

I am somewhat taken aback by the short of her tight black skirt against the length of her green sweater, but I get over the shock just in time to hand over the package and tell her what's inside. She thanks me, places her hand along my upper arm, yes, her hand along my upper arm, her hand stop motion along my clothed upper arm, a gesture of appreciation, of supreme welcome. A thank you, and a you're welcome.

I decide in that moment to be welcome today, to show my welcome into the world of Marieke as her world collides with mine along ancient footpaths destroyed by fire and ash. Pompeii, we leave Michelangelo behind to find you. Destruction and trauma will join our smiles together, a gesture of fantasy, a nonchalant touch to the cloth that covers the skin of my upper arm. I look her in the eyes and say quietly, Shall we go?

I AM ON a bus. I sit near the front for proximity's sake, to measure my aggravation by the rhythm of Marieke's bated breath. I am determined to feel enthusiasm and exuberance today, determined to show her how little her defection has done, despite the hole in the wall of my bathroom two days ago and the prize hidden in my suitcase.

She speaks to the bus driver in Italian simply to avoid my eavesdropping. Murderous jealousy. I force myself into a self-imposed exile of internal monologue. The question I ask myself is a philosophical one, not even very clever, just to establish myself on a higher intellectual plane than she will ever reach. Mind/body dualism, how can it be presented in visual form when the body and mind must be one to perform an act of creation? Does the act of creation need a body, need a mind? What is the minimum required to render a creator an artist? The theory of aesthetics feels solid and gaping as I consider the way the light falls on the tip of her thumb.

I take my phone out of my ragged handbag to check the time, see a message from Marcel. At that moment, I remember his face, the inflection of grey hair at his temples, always absolutely appropriate to his gaze. I sent him a message last night: One more day. He tells me that the kids can't wait to see me, that they've almost finished filming their movie, that it's spectacular, that he hopes I'm having a good time with the tour guide, that I'd better come home with good stories.

How might I force the moment to its crisis for his entertainment? How can I be both Prufrock and the women, both Highsmith and the murdered lover? I am a cat's paw curled into an afternoon nap.

I respond with a brief message telling him to give the kids a hug for me, wish me luck with the tour guide. She's playing hard to get and can't be trusted.

Richard sits just across the aisle commenting on Italian road signs. He attempts to translate the signs into Latin, and then for fun translates his commentary. He says, Who can say what the law should be? The translation proves difficult and many faceted. His monologue: Quis locuafor quid leges sint? Quid leges sint? Quis locuator? No. Quis possit dicere quid leges sint? Wait a minute. Quis leges sint? Quid leges. Who can say what the law should be. Who can say. What would it be. Who can say. Quis locquator. No. Quis decat. Quis decat quid leges sint. Yes. That would be it. Quis decat quid leges sint.

Marieke smiles into her voice, Richard, you are ready for Pompeii.

Helen repeats Quis decat and writes the phrase down in her tiny red notebook, remembers her college Latin teacher who helped her write her graduate school application statement, who laughed in hearty tones at our mistakes and loved the sound of chalk taping on the board at the front the class, who told Helen once she should call her if she ever needed a university post.

The ride to Pompeii is long, flat, yellow. I pass the time writing in my notebook imagined conversations about the novel I'll write describing this trip, the awards and accolades. Helen will be rewarded for not committing her animosity to language, hand to mouth, leg to thigh, teeth to neck on a bus ride.

The bus stops several hours later, Marieke makes a few unnoticed announcements, and we step down into the cool sunny air next to a flea market scene, stalls where tourists like the Texans will spend a good amount of money.

The air chills my blue sweater and dark denim pants. Tarpaulin awnings echo me back to childhood fairgrounds and picnic family reunions. The men who work the stalls call out to me in English, Miss, and Did you see this, and I'll give you a discount. They want to lure me into detritus, plastic graveyards, phallic sculpture replicas of those found in Pompeii's secret room. The phalluses of Pompeii become quite the attraction for the

Texans. I hear their gravelling voices while I decide I must find a toilet soon.

I find a discreet restroom guarded by two older women. I give them two Euros, they say welcome sweetheart, use the toilet as you'd like. They sit so close they can hear the sound of my urination.

I leave the toilet, awkward smile, then stroll with mild fascination at the endless bouquet of manufactured goods. Marieke appears alongside me, asks if I'm going to buy anything. I tell her No, I'm not a big shopper, tell her all these phalluses are quite tempting, however. She smiles and begins a long diatribe against capitalistic consumption, says it's one of her least favorite aspects of the job, to peddle worthless merchandise on behalf of these sellers who have made deals with travel companies and the tour participants who would be angered if we didn't make such stops.

I tell her about my own moves toward minimalism, lament the fact that that experience seems only wrapped round what can be bought and sold. She says, We both don't shop, then. We have a similar enthusiasm for many things, she says, and again I am welcomed into her intimacy, her cheek nearly next to mine, I imagine her lips just to the side of my thigh.

We stroll in solidarity until it's time to have some lunch. She gathers us all together, points to the restaurant, tells us we'll be served as a larger group before we enter the walls of the old city. She and I cross the street together.

THE RESTAURANT IS a hollowed out Italian gangster film. Checkered tablecloths, lots of light, misshapen décor haphazard on the walls, uncomfortable chairs placed at long family-style tables. The three brothers who own the place speak with Marieke in enthusiastic tones, almost shouting, wild gesticulations taken from a 1960s stereotype.

We file in, find chairs. Richard sits at the head of the table in random fashion, the waiter suggests he choose the wine and the appetizers for the whole table. We gleefully give him the task and tease him about acting the pater familias. I sit to Richard's left, Marieke sits directly across the table from me. Our feet touch under the table with surreptitious intentions.

The meal is ordered in English, pizza, pasta, seafood, and soon arrives in immense portions. We giggle at each other, imagine the inevitable leftovers. The restaurant brothers goad us into trying each other's food, pour endless glasses of wine, shout at us and each other their appreciation for our mouths and wallets.

Marieke orders a plate of seafood and revels in the quantity of shells and tentacles floating in a creamy white sauce thinned almost to broth. She shares with Richard but I tell her I have enough to deal with on my own heaping plate of pasta. We drink wine, we listen as the brothers break into Italian song, we pass water and bread around the table and look out the window at sunny bright Pompeii all around us.

My plans become tenuous as she looks at me across the table. I wonder if the Texan played chaperone last night after all, begin to feel badly for pouting at the top of the steps. She is making up with me over bowls of funny octopi and long strands of her hair. She reminds me of the glass of wine we shared a few short days ago. I marvel at her gaiety. When I smile in return, I revel in her recompense.

After lunch we all find the ticket line to a destroyed city, we stand in the shadow of a volcano that stopped Pompeiian dogs from roaming the streets.

Finally we enter, meet our tour guide, the last we will have, who escorts us over to a grassy area that feels strange and unexpected among the ashen ruins. His voice is a hum of distant insects, a slow faucet drip you only half hear, boring, monotone, a kindly middle-aged man who cannot make any of this seem exciting even to himself. He's the perfect guide, I think, truthful and superbly unimpressed. I listen intently as an affront to others who disregard him, relish every syllable, imagine his voice captured in an audio recording I listen to at night to fall asleep as he walks us through barren craggy streets of the city.

The size of the city surprises me, as does the joy Richard finds in hopping across stones used by the ancients to keep early wagon wheels in line. He steps up onto one, waits a beat, then bounds enthusiastic across to the next, a diversion, a tip of the hat to native Latin, a game to delight the young girls who now look at him rather than down at their phones.

We wander in and out of walled buildings, wait for a miraculous event of some kind or another, suspect that the presence of adolescent girls on our tour compels the guide to keep the juicy parts of town hidden. I look around for phalluses like the ones shaped by manufacturers and sold at market outside the city gates, erect, virile, overlarge, sometimes spread into an animal's anus. Perhaps these scenes cost an extra ticket fee, which I would have happily purchased.

The tour guide's drone strikes each narrow lane where faint colors have clung to the stone for thousands of years, perfect, worn, pastel, fading to crumbling, remnants of motion now rendered timeless except as seen through the mirrored glass of the human eye as it passes for a moment then vanishes.

We travel in and out of rooms and are told the utilitarian purpose of each, kitchen, storefront, bathhouse, family living space. I take out my camera, think of the walls as canvas, colored pastels at the tip of my wetted paint brush, random strokes, thickened here for texture and scratched out with a knife. The lens crafts the aesthetic I desire. I narrow in on a single overlarge white crack in an otherwise colorful wall, respite from a bore, I capture its image.

Like me the camera longs for texture. I offer it an etched flower, it craves blue so I find some nearby alongside lonely thickened orange, burned by two thousand suns, reproduced here in my hands. I give the camera what it wants, we define our relationship with flecks of colored granite, play out our love on the cold stone walls. I might remain here, burned beneath rubble in the child's playroom, wondering how they could possibly know this room without the ghost of a child to tell them.

The tour is quiet with fatigue, lonely footfalls litter the streets made of cobbles and concrete. A lock of Marieke's hair is stuck there, again, on her bottom lip, she makes no move to remove it.

My camera aches to catch the lost strand of hair, to keep it safe even as the wind picks up, even as a larger man across the way scruffs his hands to his unshaven face. I hear an airplane, desolate in its isolation, the giggle of girls looking to their phones. How to take a picture without her knowing? Where exactly to lace the camera to conceal the fact that I subjugate her body to the wishes of my own? How to avoid feeling the creep, getting caught in an act of admiration that might someday render her into art more exquisite than she could ever be without me? Yes, Helen snaps photos for this woman's posterity, for her place among muses, her own Band of Outsiders dancing in the café. Marieke, she is the girl in the dark hat who leaves the dance floor last, the lost girl roaming the streets of Paris waiting for a camera to call her into focus. She will thank me someday for rendering her into more than she is, for seeing in one strand of hair the beauty of Botticelli.

Camera tucked between my breasts, I snap, hope she is in focus. The thin of her body fills the frame, but I have missed the clasp of hair. I take another photo, a bit braver. The result is a lack of focus. The feat, I discover, requires brazen adventure, a throwing out of caution, devil may care. She will never see me again after the tour anyway.

Helen will never tire of secrets.

Finally, I hold the camera bold to my face, focus the lens, depress the shutter five times. I will choose later which is the truest and most rare image, but for now I have accomplished the feat of the voyeur.

Just around the corner and through a narrow passageway is the entrance to the ancient brothel. Our guide points out the menu of possible items and their prices, makes a point about a fast food restaurant menu, a few people laugh out of politeness.

We enter the room, noting nothing of phallic interest. Richard drafts his disappointment with a sly smirk toward Marieke, she laughs quietly, looks down at her map still amused. I feel vaguely jealous that Richard's gregarious style has her showing her teeth while my presence seems glum and in the corner.

WE RE-EMERGE INTO a dusty main street and eventually exit the walls of the old city. Vesuvius looms in the background of group photos Marieke insists we take. After suffering in a few of them, I excuse myself, wander like a somber relic as the wind tries to move my short red hair.

Before we all get on the bus back to Rome, we are given fifteen minutes to either use the restroom or purchase souvenirs from the outdoor market. I enter the doors just to the left of the lunchtime restaurant, descend the stairs to the large public restroom. The mirror greets the dappled redness of my skin, my hands instinctively move to smooth out the complexion.

Turning toward the bathroom stalls, I see on the ground a dirty white tote languishing in the centermost stall. Small white shoes. The sound of polite urination ruins me, my skin goosefleshes in the chill air. I listen, open my mouth slightly, analyze the hiss and pressure, revel in my secret espionage.

The sound empties. I rush into the stall just beside her, jacket and bag tight around my body. She entertains me by pulling up her stockings around her waist, straightening her clothes, hair falling on the sides of her body as she checks to make sure all is in order. All is in order. The mirror waits for her too just outside the door. She greets it while I unbutton my own pants and slide them down my thighs. The door opens, closes. I will sit close to her on the bus all the way back to Rome.

We all walk together to the bus, heave ourselves up the steep steps. We await the last of Marieke's silly bus games against the monotone golden sheen of Italy. I must sit close to her on this last journey, no sulking in silence in the furthest seat to the back. My warm mouth and dry hands take a seat in the very front row next to Richard, just across the aisle from Marieke.

She stares for a few moments out the window, then stands center aisle, tells us all over the microphone to settle into our seats for the long drive back to Rome. We'll be playing one last game in just a few minutes. I sit along the aisle, just next to where she will stand. Though Richard and I had planned to simply enjoy the scenery and laugh at Italian automobiles all the way back to Rome, we suppose a game could be fun as well.

The game begins as the yellow landscape searches our imaginations. Marieke takes the microphone in her hand, silences us all. Exerted voices in the back, hostile with attention, frames her eye and mouth. She describes the activity, which plays on Italian gestural communication. Italians are famous for using their hands, she says.

I see her hands covering my face, running through strands of my very short hair.

We are required to look at a picture of hands in the

form of gesture, watch her model what's on the picture, and guess the meaning behind the movement. In an absurd turn of things, the winner of each round receives a tiny specked plastic chicken. Her white tote becomes a perpetual narration.

She holds up a card, asks me to hold the folder that contains the rest and some paperwork about the tour. Helen, the voyeur, places the folder in her lap, legs electric with proximity. The game begins, she finds a winner, tosses out a prize. I am struck by surprises, words I have uttered, her unsteady feet on a moving bus.

The moment her leg touches mine I disappear into the yellow Italian sun. I was never there, I was so far gone. She steadies herself against me, her body sways in the center aisle with purpose. Her hand brushes mine when she hands me a card to place into the folder, the touch carries all the energy of the afternoon. The bus jerks, she falls on me with the whole of her hip and thigh. My eyes to hip to paper to road before me to her mouth near the small microphone. Her words, for me, only partly for others.

Hips and thighs mute the memory of home. I have yet to touch her hair. Decisions come in a leg muscle twitch while the bus turns a corner. We turn a corner, Marieke caught in the energy of two bodies touching on a rapid bus line in Italy.

The game takes longer than it should and I am her faithful helper through it all. I hand her the next card, she shows it to the laughing crowd, hands it back to me with a slight bend in the paper. My hand brushes hers in the exchange, calm, smiling with all of my teeth. I swerve to the music of the asphalt beneath us and try to read road signs here and there.

My emotions are a jumble of her leg against mine. Have I met a certainty, brought it to its knees? Shall I wear her scarf on the plane ride home tomorrow? And how shall I return? Marcel, the children, we together. The quiet, the aching noise, the jealousy and endless decisions. Marcel and I used to write together on the living room floor, read each the other's work with praise for a bright future. It made us feel better to say so.

The microphone hugs her wet lips as she again leans on my seat for balance. She ends the game by discarding the cards into my lap and announces over the speaker a Thank You for Helen, who has been her helper today. She looks down at me, a momentary signal that confirms my desperation.

We will be in Rome in a few hours. In the meantime, she has taken her seat adjacent, showing me for several hours the run in her stockings that runs up the length of her thigh.

AFTER PLAYING THE coquette with her stockings for several hours, we finally arrive back at the hotel. Her back faces me in a splendor of shape, her sweater curves to the side of her body, a slight wrap in the fabric calls my name. I dare to touch it.

Feigned cowardice gives me permission to brush the fold of her sweater with my fingertips, even look at her in the eye. I give a polite excuse me. She looks back, eye into my eye, a found look. Fabric still textures my hands as I walk away. I am off to my room to freshen for dinner. The walk is full of her skin.

I decide how to spend the fifteen minutes until we all meet for dinner. I check my face, make sure my dark eyeliner has been firmly impressed, change into a black V-neck top. I lay down on the bed and pull up my shirt, fingers to breast, resolute, my hand stops at the waistline, save this for later. I rise, descend to meet the group, hope to benefit from one last night in her orbit, her eyes toward my own.

The restaurant is a crowded mess of tour groups from all over the world. Marieke arranges for us all to be seated. Richard and I sit at a corner table with enough room for at least four more people. We both hope Marieke will join us, seated nearby with open laughter.

But she takes her time. I see her place her tote down near another table, but she does not sit down. And now here she comes to me, her feet carry her to me. She regards me, places her hands on the table, tells us that she is obliged to sit at another guest's table. A rule, she must sit with all groups at least once on the tour. I tell her with roving thoughts, that's too bad, maybe breakfast then. She says she'll try to get away for a few minutes during dinner to join us.

Without her help in ordering, I receive a dish full of meat instead of the vegetarian option. I eat it anyway, careful not to cause problems for the busy waiters. The taste is dour and full in my mouth. Richard converses with two others. I am lonely and full of repetition.

After about thirty minutes, Marieke suddenly appears with her tote and asks if she can join us for the rest of the meal. Richard pulls out her chair, she sighs a very long sigh as she sips at her glass of wine. She is only inches from me as she opens her mouth.

We chat about nothing, then, in a grand gesture she asks if we wouldn't mind if she removes her earrings at the table. They have been tugging at my hair all day, she says. I watch her move both hands to her ear, bring down the large hoops reminiscent of the 1980s. She places them there on the table, just near my glass of wine. The earrings lay within reach while we share gossip about the other tour groups, mock the way they chew their food.

The laughter is long. After a few minutes, she excuses herself to check on other guests. Come back soon, I tell her. Open flirt.

She leaves the table, then Richard speaks with others in our group as I perform a subterfuge. My hand slips over one of her earrings, just there in front of me, I slip it into my bag, rearrange the table settings somewhat, tug slightly at the tablecloth to give the appearance of a disturbance cause entirely by wine and good conversation.

She returns, says nothing of the missing jewelry.

After dinner, I leave the table before her. Perhaps she will notice it missing, I must make sure I'm not there to assist in the hunt.

Helen has decided to take for herself, to lay naked before the world, proclaim her rapacious appetite, eat sloppily and drink with her teeth showing, touch her own breasts in ravenous delight, tell no one of her accomplishment.

The walk back to the hotel becomes an exercise in bare-breathed self-revelation, in forgetting the prose to find what happens between the words.

Marieke, Richard, and I walk side by side on the long avenue. Richard uses the phrase 'tough titty' and we become a roiling gaiety of wine and food and crisp air. He explains to Marieke the meaning of the phrase, its derivation, its idiomatic purposes. When she decides to use it with tour guests, he quickly laughs her out of the idea. I smile, describe the pejorative nature of the phrase. We dwell in connotation on a Roman street corner.

She bumps her shoulder against mine, a playful knock that throws off my gait. She says she likes the way I explain things. I forget my unsightly raincoat and week's growth of underarm hair.

A SHOULDER TOUCH, a dark street, two realities simultaneously unearthed, precise concentric circles pleading with Helen to act. Reach out her hand. Point her arm in a single direction. A revelation, a disparity, Marieke's earring in my purse. The walls around Helen crumble, she is transported to a faraway dimension that appears uncannily like our own.

No expectations, only invitations. No pretense, only one last drink with her tonight. I feel my lips asking her to meet me at the hotel bar. Just us, a nightcap to discuss the art of Florence. My breath reaches her. She says Yes, I'll be down at nine. I say, This is the last night. She says, Let's make the most of it then.

On entering my room, I decide to pack before nine o'clock so the evening has a chance to breathe. I empty my suitcase, begin to replace each item in pristine order. I fold her scarf, but it decides instead to wrap itself around my body. I breathe deeply, take off my shirt, drape the fabric over my breasts, the last time I will do so in Italy, she a few rooms away. I wet my finger, run it over my chest, feel the cool air as it streaks down my skin. The scarf remains folded over me as I organize all other items. I place the scarf in last, move all other clothing to give it space at the bottom of the case.

I straighten the bed, make sure my makeup is not amiss, brush my teeth, and remove a few stray facial hairs that may offend if gotten too close.

Now is the time to go downstairs, to meet her at the bar. We will have a drink. I will invite her to my room. She will say Yes with her tongue and mouth which will then be mine behind a closed door.

The hotel bar is crowded with men in business attire and several women with faraway looks in the opposite direction. Marieke was there already, she had changed her clothes. Her shirt is sheer and black, torn lace, only almost wearing anything.

I sit down across from her, the curve of the glassy bar counter between us. She already ordered me a vodka and cranberry having remembered from several nights ago my affinity for the drink. I accept with graciousness, wink an eye at her clear flirtation. She had been consummate tour guide, now she drinks a glass of wine alongside me, her legs crossed, the long straight of them just in my sight.

She asks me if I've had a good time on the tour, says she didn't know enough about ancient Rome to make it truly amusing. I tell her the tour has been perfect, she has been perfect, even to the Texans. I say I'm impressed that you touched that Dante woman on the shoulder. She responds, I want a good tip. Apartments in Rome can be quite expensive, she says. I say, I'd love to see your apartment here in town. I'd take you there if I could, she says.

Her mouth wraps around a long drink of wine, her arms suddenly reach the end of the bar. I hear, Why don't we go back to my room and devilish smile the place up? The idiom slurs my speech in admiration.

Helen, here it happens for you, every cue has been read, reciprocal gnarled affections, one night in Rome, every note struck just right on the keyboard, both feet in the same direction. Sincerity sublimates itself to long blond hair with only one earring underneath. She takes my hand, says Let's go.

I have followed these footsteps also through Venetian restaurants, wet Florentine streets, market stalls in Pompeii.

We step into the hall, then into her room. She closes the door. Now Helen takes. She turns to Marieke, pushes her lightly against the blue door, fingers, voice, teeth. She moves two steps forward, puts her mouth squarely on the woman's lips, neck, mouth, tongues soft and slow and quivering inside each other's mouths. The door cannot hold us there. We must be closer, include our hands, her lips soft on my neck, my hands up the sheer black fabric of her shirt until the skin underneath is full and wild and buried deep within the folds of my fingers. Our mouths laugh into each other, our eyes stay open, my hands at her throat, they crawl in a gesture of giving. I stop and stare and touch and put my tongue against her shallow skin. She can't escape my hands and mouth, she cannot move except to the sound of my shifting feet, she cannot move except within me and toward my fingertips which are now parting the top of her shirt to reveal her chest. I put my mouth to her again.

The taste of salt on my tongue wrestles with my fingertips. I pull her in more deeply. Her comments about David are now only a preview of lightly bitten flesh. I punish her body for the Texan's laugh. I open her denim pants, slide my hands down slowly to meet her frame glorified in its meekness. She removes her pants with her own hands, spreads herself out on the bed. I find her mouth, hand, thighs, finger, pure white panties, I pull her breast into my mouth. Her arms overhead reveal her whole body to me. I begin a long, slow descent. My fingers inside her are the form my artistry takes, my palette her dark hair close to my mouth. I sculpt her body into my own aggression, fill her with hand and mouth. We lay, we writhe, we play, we smile, we tease, we feel, we embrace, we touch our breasts together and share our knees in the folds of the sheets, we erase memories and create them again. We bring each other to climax in sweat and warm skin and touched faces. I bury my neck into her thigh, taste the wet of her with my aching tongue. I drink her into me, put my fingers into my mouth.

We lay side by side for an hour, look at the ceiling, wondering what need there is of art.

I leave her room with my hair wet and my skin a mottled revelation. She lay still unclothed, her knee bent and one hand hanging over the bed. I tell her before I leave that she resembles a painting by Titian.

I walk the ten steps down the hall to my own room, enter and close the door, a different door than before, different lights, different shadows, even my own jacket looks to be owned by someone else. I have become an interloper in the minutia of my own life, a stranger to my glasses, keys, coins, my new leather purse has become a thing owned by a stranger I knew once but can never seem to contact again.

I turn on the French television station and cannot

understand a word. I look at my phone. A message from Marcel. A string of letters I cannot fathom. I wonder who has entered this room and replaced all my things with exact replicas. I wonder if I am the replica. Replicated Helen, a photocopy version here just to turn out the lights to go to sleep.

I reach deep inside my suitcase and find her one lost earring, then sit at the small mirrored desk, my own still reddened face looking back at me. I recognize this woman. This woman is Helen. Born of the medieval and built of her own small cell, long dark robes hold her arms when she is writing. Helen, who sees the world as a version of art, the beauty she sees is everywhere in patches of color, yellow, red, blue, the wind in Venus's hair. Florence hangs over her now, in the mirror is a work of magnificent beauty. Helen, who once pierced her navel and now pierces her ear with the sharp end of Marieke's lost jewelry. A bloodied wince, a glorious splendor of disheveled hair. Pierced ear, cry of adoration, obsession turned fantasy turned question mark turned mouth, a loose strand of hair, a sly turn of the eye, a tug at the wrist.

Blood smeared and drying down my neck, I remove all my clothes and sleep in the shadow of her scent, a long slow layered sleep fallen into immediately after checking one last time the number of hours left in the night.

Day Eight

Departure

I WAKE EARLY in the dim light, sunlight making its crowded way between the shutters and through the words I hardly have yet. The diffusion of light on light blue walls, the memory of what may have been a dream. My back an ache from walking all week, the bottom of my feet can hardly take the weight of my thick legs and torso.

Feet to the side of the bed, well before the alarm, I gather myself for a warm shower. A glance in the mirror reminds me that this very evening will not be spent in a hotel room. Tonight, the television will be full of familiar sounds. I glimpse darkened red along my neck, regret that it will be gone by the time I'm home.

In the shower, my fair skin and red hair remind me of the beaded sweat I had known just several hours prior. I wonder, how will the goodbye go today in a Roman airport surrounded by Texans? How will the narrative change when I give her a well-deserved tip? Will a melancholy air settle the morning, a veneer of sadness that will end as soon as I see my children's faces?

These questions glaze the surface of things. Only the night can handle the depth of Helen's features as they pierce and stain themselves into the world. Perhaps the real questions will present themselves on the bus ride to the airport, or as I search for classical music on the airplane music channels. Helen wonders what her thoughts even mean this morning. Most often there is some relevance, but today she can find only a single thin drip of water falling steady from her breast.

I step out of the shower onto the cool grey tiles and relive the first moments in Italy. Cold tiles, worn patchwork wallpaper, bed turned down for the next night's sleep. It is early, there is time to throw the clock in the air and catch it, to rewind, resign, time to lean against a pillar in a moment of reflection. I will remain in this room in nude splendor, riven and shaken, quiet, solitary, confirmed, transposed.

There must be some gesture possible to close out the week, period instead of an ill-placed comma. I remember the first time she touched my shoulder. I was crying over David.

A postcard. A picture postcard, which I will write and give to her before I depart. There will no contact, but there will be words, and a picture of David.

I reach into my small backpack, into the plastic bag where the gift shop postcard rests. A supreme sacrifice, an offering, a reclamation. My one postcard of the trip, the only reminder of the experience at the feet of David will be in her hands and pondered over for a moment. Each time I do not see this image hanging above my writing desk will be a moment I must have created for her. The absence will be the cue, the murder of thereness, the scales tipped toward empty, a blank spot on the wall will gesture memory transmuted into purer existence.

Now, the problem of what to write. It must be simple. It must not mention last night, the side glances and light touches under cathedral ceilings. It must be reflective, but not profound, must seem as if I wrote it down before her mouth had been known to me.

Helen, now is the time for nonchalance, don't spoil the gesture with anxiety and an empty pen. Just write the first thing that comes to your mind, no consequence, what does it matter anyway? She will look on this for a moment, then pack it away in a box of tumultuous nothings, no thought, no word, no letter will make any difference whatsoever. Be more now than an equation you don't quite understand.

I begin to write directly on the card without rehearsal or a series of drafts. If I make a mistake, I have no other card to replace it. There must be no consequence or it will never be written.

Helen writes banality and a nothing, Helen writes, Thank you, Marieke for a lovely week and for showing me David. I will be the artist looking over my shoulder for quite some time. With much fondness, Helen.

Is that enough? Will she remember our conversation, understand the import of the remark? Could she fathom the moment rolled into Prufrock's ball waiting for her at the bottom of the sea, mired in salt and crusted with vines and moss? The words are perfect, meaningful in just the way Helen likes, known mostly to herself unless the receiver delves into the abyss to find her waiting with a sentiment in her hand.

Postcard finished, packed and ready, I take the deep step out into the hotel corridor, fearful of her seeing again my belly, folds in my skin. I hope she has forgotten. Safe, no one here, just Helen alone with a suitcase in her hand and a sense of well-being in the corner of her eye. I pull my hat over head to cover my ears for self-preservation.

Early morning, down the elevator, the hotel is not yet serving breakfast. The air is quiet, I imagine sighing breaths of long sleep. A few tour mates are there waiting, Richard is there, I seek him out, tell him how happy I am that we were able to laugh and hang round on the trip. Everyone needs a trip bestie, I say. He returns a sleepy sentiment and we both begin to wonder about breakfast, merely a small white paper bag with undoubtedly paltry sustenance inside.

Marieke's long green sweater finally arrives, commands us to grab breakfast and follow her to the bus. We do, we all do. We all follow her long strides and her head turning both ways at every crossing. The bus waits around the corner to take us to the train that will bring us closer to the airport. We must walk the mile from the bus to the train station.

I try my hardest not to be remembered for last night.

The packed breakfast is minimal and none of us have had coffee. A few tour mates flirt and plead with Marieke to find coffee somewhere. She says not to worry, she knows a place inside the station.

She looks at me as she turns. I smile and do not turn my head away.

WE TRAVEL TWENTY minutes by foot to the subway that will take us to the train. Quiet subdued morning, walking along a waterway in Rome. Curious now that I don't remember there being any water in the city. Deep, large embankments obscure it from view.

We again must wait while Marieke makes her plans. My time is spent directly in a passion. The week is old, the walk is grey along the water. A dead fog has settled down around our feet, it waits for our feet to part it. We walk single file in the near darkness and comment on the fog to one another. The feeling is lonely, as if all contrast has left us here to wander resolute and unarmed toward a destination we can hardly pronounce. I put one foot in front of the other in great suspense, a necessity of blind trust that at the end of the walk there will life and a story and some brewed coffee.

Finally reaching the station, Marieke finds us a small café where we all immediately and in ravenous envy descend. I ask Marieke if she'd like anything. It's a gesture of intimacy born of a walk in the fog and a week-long voyeurism that culminated in a night of sweat and skin.

She says Yes, a Cappuccino please, and I rush to be

the first one in line to get it for her. Richard and I order together. He wants to take credit for getting her drink, but I tell him, No, I'll give it to her. He smiles, knows not to protest.

We pay, carry our drinks to the train line, which has started boarding. She waits for me, looks up from her itinerary.

We find ourselves inside a long, darkened cabin, solemn day, much reminiscing. I finally eat my paper bag breakfast, soft cheese and dry crusty toast, an apple, some grapes. My coffee drinks in the last day.

One of the older women in our group asks after the whereabouts of a younger girl named Grace. She is not with her friends, who are looking for her as well. We all go on the hunt, worries she may have been left behind. Richard looks toward the front of the train. I wander the aisles alongside passengers dining. A young girl lost, a final day's disappearance. Perhaps she too met her Marieke, perhaps she too started in hopes of finding a work of art to stare back at her, perhaps she has found a young cleric who drew her into a life of devout anticipation, a world where belief exists. A lost young girl, a found Helen with cheese in her pocket and wandering eyes.

I go back to my seat to see if Richard has had any luck. Along the way, there, in an adjacent sitting area, somehow cold like the wind has found its way to us, I see Marieke's face and yellow hair. Her green jacket lingers as if in an open-air seat. She sits next to a young girl who I assume is the lost one, talking, not talking, simply existing in solidarity. Marieke finds lost girls in their hiding places and brings them out to play.

We eventually arrive at the airport in a frenzy of tired clichés, the day still barely lit, the sun hides from the morning.

We all descend tired and full of fatigued quips about the price of souvenirs at airports. I stand near to Marieke after I retrieve my suitcase and talk about how quickly the tour managed to be over even though at the start it felt like it would go on for ages. She says she feels the same way, that later in the week she'll be leaving Rome for good to return to her mother and father in the Netherlands.

I also return home today, a family of young artists waits for me.

She and I are unaware of the full extent to which the other's life has tangible outcomes, other eyes that pierce our skin. She walks forward to help one of the Texans with her oversized suitcase just as I put my fingertips to my swollen earlobe to comfort the pulsing ache.

Inside the airport is warmth and the smell of ammonia, a grand escape filled with looming deadlines and worried faces. All of us stand in line at the ticket counter, lazy and alone, to hand off our luggage. The need for food by this time leaves me in a flushed absence despite the clarity of the fluorescent lights above. My flight leaves in three hours, there will be time to eat, to wander sullen. I look around for Marieke, she stands at the back of the room, waiting arms crossed, turning her head from side to side to get the best view of all of us.

I feel my phone in my pocket vibrate, open it to see a message from Marcel. He and the kids can't wait for my return, he says, and they have a surprise for me when I get home. My eyes fill with anticipation and my faraway journey. Marcel and the kids, far from me, so little to do with this airport, with a green sweater, with images in my camera that will tell a story they have not read.

I can find nothing to say but the banal, yet again. I can't wait to see them too, can't wait for the surprise, tell the kids I love them and look forward to seeing their movie.

All of this is true. Also true is the fact of Marieke's touch one solitary Roman night.

THE TEXANS AND a few others in the group leave earlier than Richard, me, and all the younger girls, so Marieke asks us to wait for her while she makes sure they get through their security checks. She looks at me, says, Will you wait for me? I tell her we will all be right here waiting before she disappears.

We sit, talk a little, I stand up and wander a few feet away as if looking at the airport map. Truthfully, though, I desire solitude just now, to be seeped in melancholy, no other voices to breathe in the delicious air of nostalgia for moments that have not yet passed, to feel the isolation of being unknown and apart, distant from the music of the everyday, lost deep within the space between my own secret walls.

Helen alone, Helen alone. Helen alone in a brightly lit airport tunnel, Helen stranded in time in a black coat and hat. There are routines to be managed, yes, but just now Helen will know the beating of her own heart.

She takes a long time, or rather it seems a long time to Helen as she watches from her desperate reverie. How can she say what she has felt, the anger, jealousy, desire, possession, hollow lips, empty hands, David's eyes? How shall Helen create, how shall her waking moments be spent with a pen in her hand, glasses removed from her face? How shall she feel the aches in her wrist from writing so many letters, each one resembling one of Marieke's light freckles? How shall she find reprieve in her own space with a notebook out before her? It's a future Helen can see but cannot find. She fears it all might be left at David's feet, or near the exit to the Sistine Chapel.

Marieke finally returns, tells us it's time to get to our gates for the long trip home. She gives her well wishes to Richard and the girls, hugs and Keeps in Touches as they make their way to the security line. I linger behind with a postcard in my hand, and an envelope with a significant tip. Shyness suddenly approaches as I consider the last moment, I take my feet toward her nonetheless.

Marieke, I say, I have something for you, to remind you of your superior understanding of Michelangelo's power. She sees the picture on the postcard, accepts the envelope with a gracious Thank You. We hug lightly, as if our bodies had not been inside each other's just a few hours ago, as if only the past says to the other, your skin tasted sweet in my mouth.

I say, well, goodbye then, and she says we must keep in touch. I say, yes, of course, we should, realize it is time to turn away.

Before I allow my feet to move, I lift my arm to her

shoulder, allow my fingertips to touch a curl buried in her long hair. I smile, say It was a magical trip, and now it is time to go home.

I turn away from her, see the line of fellow travelers deep into their own goodbyes, and walk toward them with unclear steps and a forward motion. The first steps I have taken, the last ones I will take here.

As I turn the corner, she is now out of sight. Even if I looked back now, she would not be there. I look back anyway, see the swollen morning outside the window. The sun has finally made its way to me.

I put finger to pulsing earlobe, feel a slow trickle of blood from the reddened wound. There must be a way to remedy this, I think, as I see drops of blood diffuse themselves over my hand.

I look in my bag for a cloth of some sort, but only find a crumpled, forgotten piece of notebook paper, lonely with no words. This will do. I place it to my ear, stain it red. Lined paper and a drop of blood, they leave Helen behind as she marches out silent into the light of day.

Printed in the USA
CPSIA information can be obtained
at www.ICGtesting.com
CBHW011143290324
6072CB00024B/2106